George Ware Briggs, John Fisk Allen

Memorial of Pickering Dodge Allen

George Ware Briggs, John Fisk Allen

Memorial of Pickering Dodge Allen

ISBN/EAN: 9783337093853

Printed in Europe, USA, Canada, Australia, Japan

Cover: Foto ©Raphael Reischuk / pixelio.de

More available books at **www.hansebooks.com**

MEMORIAL

OF

PICKERING DODGE ALLEN.

BY HIS FATHER.

———— ◄◄•►► ————

BOSTON:

PRINTED BY HENRY W. DUTTON AND SON,

90 & 92 Washington Street.

1867.

So nigh is grandeur to our dust,
   So near is God to man
When Duty whispers low, THOU MUST,
   The youth replies, I CAN.

RALPH WALDO EMERSON.

MEMORIAL.

PICKERING DODGE ALLEN was born in Salem, Massachusetts, May twentieth, 1838. He attended some of
our private schools during the earliest years of his life.
Having suffered from scarlet fever, and a very severe
relapse, which confined him for many months, on his
partial recovery he renewed his studies under private
instructors, as he lost time by this illness; and not
having a particular desire for a college education, he
continued these private lessons for many years, even
to the time when he commenced his travels in this
country, preparatory to a foreign tour. As boy and
young man, he exhibited decided military taste; and
he was much interested in our volunteer militia and
held a commission in the Salem Light Infantry, which
he resigned to go abroad. His favorite reading was
that of the lives of military heroes, of battles and of
war. His memory was retentive; and I have been
often surprised, in conversation with him, to hear how

1*

familiar and thorough he was in these matters,—unusually so for one not especially educated and intended for a military life. The thought that he ever would have occasion to fight for the maintenance of the honor and independence of the flag of his country had never, up to this time, entered his mind.

Early in November, 1859,—then being nearly twenty-one years and six months of age,—he sailed from New York, in the steamer Baltic, for San Francisco, meaning to visit that region and go thence to the East Indies. What were his experiences, and what places he sojourned at, will appear by extracts from his letters :—

LETTERS FROM SAN FRANCISCO.

STEAMER BALTIC, AT SEA, Nov. 12, 1859.

DEAR FATHER,—

We have had a very fine passage, so far, and expect to arrive at the Isthmus to-night. The sail down New York harbor was very pleasant. We passed the Northern-Light steamer—the rival boat—before getting beyond the islands. The second day out, we encountered a severe northeast gale, which lasted thirty-six hours. I was seasick during this time, but have not been since. T—— was not seasick. Only nine of one hundred and fifty cabin passengers appeared at table the day of the storm. While it lasted, we had several accidents on board : One steerage passenger broke his leg, and another his arm; one of the horses died; and the planks around the wheelhouse were torn up by the sea. Among other things on board are forty-three hives of bees, and they are very plenty on the deck; they do not sting; they came very near going overboard in the storm, but most of them were saved by the sailors. I like the sea as well as I expected; it is rather tiresome. We have ten hundred and twenty-seven passengers—one hundred and fifty first-cabin, two hundred second, and the rest steerage; many extremely pleasant people among them. A lady (with her father), going to Lima, is very accomplished; she speaks six languages. Mr. Warren, of New York, is very entertaining; he has written two or three books on South America. Other Boston and New York gentlemen and ladies I have become acquainted with; and Mr. Hovelley, who is going to Panama, is a son of the President of the Panama and Aspinwall Railroad. He introduced me to the Captain, Purser, and others. The Purser offered to look after my baggage, which is a great relief, as the heat in the baggage room is intense. Mr. Crosby of Boston, and of the firm of Crosby & Co. of Callao, introduced me yesterday to a niece of my French teacher, Mons. Jerome of Salem. She wondered that you had a son so old as myself. Yesterday, we passed by Cuba without stopping; the island appeared beautiful; we were very near the shore for three or four hours. Flying fish are plentiful, but none have come on board. The weather is now extremely hot.

STEAMSHIP SONORA, NOV. 19, 1859.

I am now writing this to leave at Acapulco, as it will reach you a steamer sooner than a letter mailed at San Francisco. We arrived at Aspinwall last Saturday, at midnight,—a week ago to-day. The trip over the Isthmus was delightful, the weather being remarkably fine and the scenery grand. I was much struck with the vegetation: the trees were very large and splendid; orchids were growing on nearly all of the large ones, and some of the flowers were beautiful. Oranges, cocoanuts, bananas and pineapples were plenty; the latter remarkably fine, the oranges were not. T—— left at Panama, and has gone to Lima. Last night we had a heavy gale of wind in the Gulf of Tehauntepec, which is noted for its gales; the Captain says he never knew it blow harder on this coast; many of the ladies were much frightened, the waves were tremendous, and I was a little seasick. The blacks at Aspinwall and Panama were plenty, and willing to carry baggage at exorbitant rates; we paid them about half they asked. One of them was much delighted by a new ten cent piece I paid him; another immediately came to know if I had been to the place where they made bits; another was looking over a picture book that a child had, and seemed much pleased. Only one alligator made his appearance: he was about three feet long, and seemed nearly all mouth. We should have been at Acapulco to-night; we were detained a little by the gale; expect to be there early to-morrow, when we shall stop a few hours. The coast of Mexico—looking finely, high and bold—is now in sight. We have just passed through an immense school of porpoises; some of their jumps were wonderful. Flying fish are very plenty and are amusing, jumping in and out of the water. The steamer is very crowded; there are three in our state room; I have the middle berth. We have very pleasant times on the ship; the party well acquainted sit together at meals; we break-fast at eight and a half, lunch at one, dine at four and a half. The last of this letter has been written on my knee, and I do not know that you will be able to read it; but the table was wanted and I had to leave the saloon; even there it is hard writing, as the motion of the boat is great.

SAN FRANCISCO, DEC. 4, 1859.

We arrived in this city last Sunday; it was a splendid day. All our arrivals were on Sunday,—at Aspinwall, Panama, Acapulco, and at this place. Acapulco is a small Mexican town, with a population of about two thousand; we arrived there at two in the morning, when several gen-tlemen and myself went on shore and breakfasted on broiled chickens and fried bananas; the women who waited upon us at the table were all smoking. As soon as we landed a great number of children surrounded us, teasing us to buy all sorts of nicknacks; as we would not buy, they wanted to make presents, which we also firmly refused to accept; some who did take them were followed and had to reciprocate by giving them a half dollar, a sum much in excess in value of the article received. Fruit was plentiful and good; it was both nicer and cheaper than at Aspinwall or Panama. As soon as it was daylight the steamer was surrounded by men, swimming; they were waiting for dimes to be thrown over; their diving was wonderful, they only lost one out of a large number tossed them. The passage up from Acapulco was very pleasant; we had only one rainy day. We had one accident: a little girl of six years of age fell from the upper deck down into the second cabin, a distance of thirty feet; she broke her thigh, but the surgeon says she will get well. I am at the Oriental Hotel, a very old looking wooden building, but a very good and well kept house. The gentlemen here have been very polite and attentive: Mr. Low introduced me to the Merchants' Exchange, and his brother George to the Mercantile Library; Dr. Bonic sent me an invitation to the Pacific Club Rooms, and invited me to his house; yesterday I called on George Ward, who introduced me to gentlemen at the Union Club, and sent me an invitation to it and also one to dine there to-morrow. This city is a very singular place; the buildings being mostly wooden. The evening after we arrived quite a fire took place in the Chinese portion of the city, and the excitement among them was great; there are between five and six thousand of them in the town. There are some fine buildings, and many in course of construction. The view from Telegraph Hill— which has an elevation of six hundred feet—is splendid. I am to visit the forts at Fort Point with some of the officers stationed here; they are not yet completed, but when finished are expected to be good, and well adapted for the protection of the city. I shall remain here until M—— arrives, in the next steamer, when we shall go into the country for about ten days. The grapes here are from

Los Angelos; they are cheap, quite small and very good. I write in great haste.

SAN FRANCISCO, DEC. 18, 1859.

Your letter arrived safely, by the last steamer; she was two days behind the other boat. M—— came, and I find him a very pleasant companion. To-morrow we are going to Sacramento; then to Grass Valley and to other mining places near there. The country is now looking beautifully, about the same as in the middle of May at home; the wild flowers are commencing to bloom. I have been riding on horseback nearly every day the last fortnight, and have seen the country around here thoroughly. Many of the shops and all the theatres are open here on Sunday. M—— and myself went to Albatross Island with Lieutenant McPherson, in his boat; he has charge of the fort building there. We have been to the Presidio, where two or three hundred troops are stationed, and to Fort Point, on which is a very fine fort. We went over it with Lieutenant Elliot, who is from Billerica, in Massachusetts. The city has been quite gay the last week with a Fair in Music Hall, which was crowded all the time. The great attraction the last few days has been the encampment of the Pitt-river Indians, who were taken prisoners a few weeks ago. They left here yesterday for Mendicino, the Indian Reservation. They were a very mild looking set, and numbered a few less than five hundred; when they came, many of them had no clothing excepting a blanket, most of the children not having even that; quantities of clothes were sent them, and

before they left they looked quite respectable. Many of the
men had gold rings through their noses, which were highly
ornamental. They were not like the Indians we see at home:
they seemed docile and more easily managed, and were in
charge of a small guard. I have been out to Captain
Macondry's Ranch: it is twenty-one miles from town, and
a very pretty place; trees are plenty there, and as they are
scarce in the city it was quite pleasant to see them again.
I have dined with Mr. Ward often, at the club; he is a
very small man, and when we walk together people stare
tremendously; he suffers from the gout, which he says he
now fights off with strong coffee. The weather is remarkable, only one rainy day in the three weeks I have been here;
white frosts nearly every morning, but no ice; it is colder
up in the country. There is now only one vessel fitting for
China—the Early Bird; she is small, and sails about the
fifth of January; we shall not go in her if there is any
prospect of any other conveyance in a reasonable time. I
have at last found Ellen; she was very glad to see me:
I went again to the place where she used to live, and met
a little girl,—she knew Mrs. O'Keefe's young ones, and from
her I found her whereabouts; she now lives in an entirely
different part of the city; she is very well, and I have sent
my clothes to her to-day. My love to Marion and Lizzie.

SAN FRANCISCO, JAN. 4, 1860.

On the day that I wrote you last we left here for Sacramento, arriving there the next morning. As yet it is a
small place, well laid out. Early the next day we took the

boat for Marysville, seventy-five miles up the river. It was a thick day, and we saw but little to interest excepting General Sutler's plantation, which is a nice farm. We took the stage coach at six o'clock the next morning for Nevada, arriving there at four in the afternoon; the day was pleasant, and the drive was quite interesting; we passed through Smartsville, Timbuctoo and Grass Valley, all of them mining towns; as to the roads and the hills, they were dreadful,— nothing in New Hampshire or Vermont can compare with them. We remained three days in Nevada, examining the different kinds of mining. The proprietor of the hotel took us to the mines and introduced us to the head workman, and he took great pains to show and explain all the extensive operations: these were interesting and well worth seeing; large hills have been cut away to find the gold, and some tunnels are three hundred feet below the surface of the ground; we procured some very pretty specimens of quartz, although the gold does not show much. On our return we left at half past one in the morning, in the stage coach, called here a mud wagon; it was dark and rained hard for some hours; it cleared at sunrise; before, it was dull and stupid and tedious, many times the wagon had to stop for part of the passengers to get upon the steps and side to prevent the thing from upsetting. We reached Sacramento at three in the afternoon and remained until two in the afternoon of the next day,—arriving at San Francisco at ten that night, fairly fatigued and tired out. Your letter arrived last night—the mail steamer being eight days behindhand. The weather continues very fine, with but few storms; when it rains it pours, and floods the streets in a very short

2

time; we do not wear or need overcoats. I hope we shall be able to get away for China soon; although we are enjoying ourselves here very much we ought not to stay much longer. The city is very gay: on Tuesday we had a large party in the house, given to the guests; the next night we were at a private party given by a lady; on Friday night, to a ball at Virginia Block, and last night at a small party at Dr. Bonie's; and to-morrow, a lady in the house is to give a very large ball—over four hundred invitations have been issued. I send this by the overland mail, and, since I have been writing, the ship Don Quixote has arrived, and if she goes to China it will be a fine vessel for us to take passage there, as she is a large clipper vessel.

SAN FRANCISCO, JAN. 16, 1860.

We are to leave here on Saturday or Sunday for Japan. M—— and myself go over with Mr. Frank Knight, of Boston, who has chartered the barque What Cheer, of four or five hundred tons, with remarkably fine accommodations for passengers. Mr. Knight came from there only six weeks ago, and expects to establish a commercial house at Kanagawa. This is only a few miles from Jeddo, which place we hope to be able to visit; but this is extremely doubtful. A steamer runs from Kanagawa to Shanghai, and we expect to go to China on her. T—— has not yet arrived, and we shall probably not see him; we have been here much longer than we intended.

JAN. 23.—We are still in this city, but certainly sail to-morrow, at ten o'clock; we have three more passengers on the What Cheer—six in all. We expect to arrive in Japan about the first of March and remain about three weeks, and then go to Shanghai or Hong Kong if possible. We shall not tarry long in China if an opportunity offers for Manila, where I expect to stay about one month, and thence go to Calcutta or Batavia. You had better direct letters after the middle of March to Calcutta. I have had an attack of rheumatism, but am now well again; it lasted five days.

LETTERS FROM JAPAN.

KANAGAWA, JAPAN, MARCH 16, AND YOKUHAMA, JAPAN, APRIL 10, 1860.

DEAR FATHER AND MOTHER,—

After a pleasant passage of forty days from San Francisco we arrived off the Bay of Jeddo at sunset, and had to wait for daylight before entering. With daylight came a head wind, which soon increased so as to be blowing a furious gale, and instead of landing that day, as we had anticipated, we were blown about in nearly every direction for five or six days, when we finally succeeded in getting to the anchorage, it snowing fast at the time. When six days from San Francisco we saw two ships and spoke one—the Oracle, of New York, a fine clipper of large size; it was full moon and early in the evening, and she made a beautiful appearance. When off the Sandwich Islands we met with a severe gale, that lasted two days, and prevented our stopping for water and provisions. We did not regret this, as our stop would necessarily have been very short. The scenery

of Jeddo is quite fine,—the Bay full of junks, mostly small
fishing vessels ; and when we were sailing up the crews
saluted us with their Japanese cry of welcome. From the
anchorage the town is a very ordinary looking place,—the
houses which one sees being occupied by fishermen and
boatmen.   The Custom House is a large wooden, good
looking building, with a roof of red tiles and in a large
enclosure with a wall six or eight feet high around it.   This
country has much to interest us.   Kanagawa is an old town,
the streets very narrow; all the Consuls live here, but most
of the business is conducted at Yokuhama, two miles from
Kanagawa.   It is almost impossible to get into Jeddo, no
foreigners being allowed to go only ten miles inland.   Our
Vice Consul, Mr. Hall, has been there and remained some
weeks.   He says it is exactly like Yokuhama, only very much
more extended.   I wish very much to go there, and shall if
possible ; it is fourteen miles from here.   The walk between
Kanagawa and Yokuhama is an extremely pretty one,—the
country beautiful and the soil rich; it must be a fine place
for agricultural purposes; the camalia trees are now in full
bloom.   The people are very curious; they follow us about,
examining our clothes ; they were much pleased with my
rubber suit ; they are extremely polite and wonderfully
good natured; if we go into a store and remain an hour or
two, giving them a great deal of trouble and without making
any purchases, they seem as well pleased as with a good
customer, and always invite you to come again.   The country is densely populated ; the people are very much amused
at my height, and a great many come up and measure
themselves by me and seem to consider it a very good joke;

the men and unmarried women have very handsome teeth,—the married women blacken theirs, which makes them very homely. The boatmen are wonderfully tough; most of them wear no clothes below the knee; they do not row, but scull their boats,—the government boats having each a dozen or more scullers, each man standing up to his work; they move through the water rapidly. Very few of the people wear hats, and those that are worn are made of straw or paper, shaped like a wash basin; their umbrellas are made of oiled paper, and their stockings are made like our mittens; their shoes are kept in place by a string, passing between the toes. The streets are crowded with people, and the coolies do all the work; they draw the wagons—an ordinary cart, and four of them will take a heavy load; they make a tremendous noise, singing to keep time in working. Storks and crows are esteemed as sacred, and they are very abundant and tame; the latter would frequently alight upon our vessel, when we were aboard of her in the harbor. The Custom-house officers and petty officials wear one sword; the relatives of princes wear two, one very long, the other much shorter. The common people seem favorably disposed towards foreigners, but the princes, who have large trains to support, are much opposed, doubtless in consequence of the foreign demand for goods, which has greatly increased the cost of many articles, and made it very difficult for them to maintain their establishments. Some of these have ten thousand soldiers, clothed mostly in silk, which is, in consequence of this foreign demand, already increased in price one half. All the murders have been committed by their followers, and no doubt by their command,—the murderer

2*

escaping into the Provinces, and the Government, if they
had the will, have not the power to punish them. The lives
of foreigners are very insecure and we all go well armed.
Two Dutch captains were killed the last of February, and
cut to pieces in the main street of Yokuhama at five or six
o'clock in the afternoon, and the men escaped, although there
must have been hundreds near at the time. The next month
the followers of the Prince of Matte assassinated the Prime
Minister for the reason of his favoring the foreigners, and
had not the Governor of a Province favorable to the Government have come up at that time the assassins would have
escaped. They were all taken; had it been otherwise, a civil
war would probably have followed, as these Princes have
an army nearly as large as that of the Emperor. The
Governor of Kanagawa and Yokuhama passes through the
streets daily, on his way to the Custom House; he is a good
looking man, and has about forty attendants, several of them
being two-sworded officers; a little in advance is one man
with a long pole with iron rings; this he shakes to announce
the Governor, and as he passes all the people kneel; he usually rides on a horse, but never moves faster than a walk,
as this would not be dignified. This Custom House is a
great annoyance to us foreigners, as we have to go there
twice a day to get the small sum of ten dollars changed into
Japanese itsalves; these are worth about thirty-five cents.
The Government have been stamping Mexican dollars at
three itsalves each, but the natives will not take them at any
better rate than before, and sell their goods for much less
when paid in their currency. One great difficulty in trading
with them is that they have no fixed price, asking two or

three times as **much for an article as** they finally will sell for. I shall send home some of the porcelain, bronze and lacquered goods; these things are kept for sale in separate shops; they are very handsome. The porcelain vases are very graceful and superior to the Chinese, but having too much glass in their composition gives them a bluish color; the lacquered articles are in great variety and splendid, and the bronzes are fine.

Yokuhama has been built the last year, and here **the** business of the merchants is mostly conducted. It is regularly laid out; the main street is wide, good looking and very clean. **The houses are most** of them two stories high, the **lower story** being used for stores; they are built of wood and part of them are painted, but they are all new **and** fresh; the windows are made of strong paper, oiled; they admit a good light and wear well. We saw many handsome birds at a menagerie here, and two storks nearly as tall as myself. **Entire suits** of water-proof clothing, **of** paper, are made **here, and can be had, with a cap and** cape, for about **seventy-five cents,** the **collars being of silk;** they are glazed with oil, and are very serviceable. **We found eight or ten** English, Dutch and American **vessels here, and one Russian corvette; also one** hundred **and fifty for**eign residents, who have been **here only** a few weeks, the **most** of them,—the port was only opened last July. The Consuls all live in Kanagawa; **usually** they occupy an old Budhist Temple; General Dorr, the **American** Consul, has one particularly **well situated, on the top of a** hill, with a grove of large **trees near.** It is built of stone, and is very large; **the top of the principal room is inlaid with different** woods, finely polished and carved. The mountain Fusiana is a glorious sight at sunrise; it is nearly thirteen thousand feet high, and is now covered with snow; it seems very near, but it is more than thirty miles distant. The Japanese esteem this mountain as sacred, and have the belief that a bad man cannot ascend to its top,—that although his feet may move, he can make no progress. The Custom-house officers, being two-sworded men—petty nobility—are very proud, but fond of dining with the foreign merchants and always come in when they feel inclined, and, as the foreigners sometimes invite the Japanese merchants, they occasionally meet, when the merchant has to leave, bowing all the time to the officer, who generally takes no notice of him. We expect to sail from here for China in the Boston ship Judge Shaw, to leave near the middle of April. I have met Mr. Stearns, who was in the same house with Charles Orne for several years. He says that he is in Canton, and I shall go there to see him.

LETTERS FROM CHINA.

HONG KONG, CHINA, MAY 9, 1860.

We arrived yesterday, and on going on shore I find that the mail closes this morning and I have only time to say that we had a rather long passage of twenty-six days. The first week out from Japan we had nothing but calms and gales of wind; one of these was a typhoon, in which the ship lost all the sails set except the fore top-sail, which fortunately only split; after this we had very fine weather and light winds. Hong **Kong is** crowded with strangers; the French and English armies are encamped here; they number about forty thousand men. The harbor **is** very full of vessels—nearly two hundred ships—sixty **of** them men **of war** and transports; and the streets are entirely full of soldiers, sailors and Chinamen. The soldiers are reviewed three times a week, and the Sheik's cavalry attract much attention. **We shall go to** Canton next week, and probably **to Manila in** a Spanish **vessel of war—that takes** passengers—in about a fortnight.

MACAO, MAY 19, 1860.

Since writing you last I have been in Canton, and yester-day arrived here. When in Hong Kong M—— and myself had our quarters at the club. The great attraction there now is the army, which **is** encamped **on the shore directly** opposite the city; the reviews receive much attention, **and** the Indian Sheik's cavalry are well worth seeing; **I see by** the papers that more than half of them went north recently. Here there is great difference of opinion as regards the fighting in prospect, many thinking **that** the Chinese will not fight, **and** the residue believing that it will be very severe. Hong Kong has quite an American or European look; the houses, many **of them, are** three stories in height, and built of stone; the **Queen's road is a** handsome wide street, about a mile long. The weather is cool, and we have had no inconvenience from heat.

We went to Canton in an American steamer, and were only ten hours on the passage. At Canton I found Charles-Orne, and he invited me to remain at his house while there. He looks well and is in good health, and was very polite, taking us to see all the wonders of the city: the temples, with their gilded gods, life size,—the pagoda is very old and tall, but far from handsome; at the Temple of Congesity were quite a number of Chinese at their worship of the gilded gods (these were, some of them, ten feet high); we went to the porcelain and ivory warehouses, and found the former not so handsome as the Japanese and much more expensive; the river near the city is covered with small boats called san pans, the covered part of which is not more than six feet square, yet the number of people living in them is estimated as near one million. The merchants are living in comfort; they breakfast at ten and dine at seven or eight.

Friday morning we left Canton and arrived here this afternoon. This is the Newport of China, and a very pleasant place; we are staying with Mr. Devens of Charlestown. We have visited a Chinese theatre and enjoyed it much; the dresses were gorgeous, and fire crackers were extensively used.

SUNDAY, MAY 20.—This is my birthday and I begin to feel quite old. To-morrow we go to Hong Kong, and expect to sail for Manila on Thursday, in a Spanish Government vessel which carries the mail.

HONG KONG, 21ST.—We have just arrived here, and find the Manila vessel sails in two or three hours, three days before her usual time. I have enjoyed China very much, and should have been better pleased could we have had the few days more time here.

LETTERS FROM MANILA.

MANILA, JUNE 2, 1860.

On arriving here last week I was very glad to find five letters from you and three from other friends; two of them had been sent by way of China. M—— is with Russell & Sturgis; I am, of course, with Mr. T——. We are enjoying our visit here; we drive every afternoon and sometimes in the morning, and so many carriages and horses are kept (every gentlemen having them), and frequenting one drive every day, from six to seven in the afternoon, that guards are placed to prevent their passing each other,—the fine for doing so being ten dollars. The passage over from China was very uncomfortable, the accommodations exceedingly poor, the state rooms hot and unventilated; but on shore we do not find the heat uncomfortable, and, as this is called one of the warmest months in the year, hope it will not be so bad as we had feared. I should prefer this island for a residence to China, as the society is good, and the drives are a great advantage and the climate fine. This city has a population of about two hundred thousand, and is quite large, with many old churches and convents. The Government maintains quite a large force—now ten thousand soldiers— and the many regimental bands of music are very good, playing in different parts of the city. The Spanish boy Benigno, who went to Mr. Very's school with me, in Salem, is now in the country; he is expected to be here next week, when I hope to meet him.

I want you to send me, to Constantinople, a traveller's letter of credit, to be used there and in Europe; also my letters to the same place. We shall have to return to Hong Kong from here, and shall go by the next mail—two weeks hence—and take the regular steamer to Singapore and go from there to Batavia, as every one we see recommends us to go to Java and pass a few weeks; from there we shall go to Calcutta. I shall send home, from Hong Kong, my Japanese purchases, with a few Chinese articles. I have bought some goods here and shall send them, with most of my white clothes from Calcutta. These accumulate, and I have now twenty suits of linen and cotton, and it is hard to get along with these.

My love to M—— and L——, and all the family.

MANILA, JULY 1, 1860.

Since writing you last I have been in this city, with the exception of a few days at Masekeno, a small village ten miles from here with excellent bathing and walking facilities. The country is pretty, and the view from a high hill is a very fine one and very extensive. Yesterday we were very much surprised at T——'s arrival from Hong Kong. He will go with us to Batavia.

We expected to leave here to-morrow, but owing to some accident to the Manila boat we shall be detained another fortnight. I am sorry for this, as I do not like to spare so much time for one place. It has rained most of the time for a week past, but it is fine to-day; it is to be hoped that the rainy season is not setting in yet awhile.

LETTERS FROM SINGAPORE.

SINGAPORE, AUG. 3, 1860.

I am now on board the ship Singapore, and a few miles from the port; we expect to be at anchor soon, and, as the mail leaves the next day, write now. We left Manila on the nineteenth of July; arrived at Hong Kong in five days, after a fine, pleasant passage. As fellow passenger, we had the French Bishop of Cochin China, a very agreeable man, and we talked in French, which was at least advantageous to me. We have a French officer in this ship, so that I have been able to keep up conversation as well as if Mons. Jerome had been with us. I hope to be so fortunate as to meet with more on the future passages at sea. Before leaving Manila, we were present at the inauguration of a statue of the Queen of Spain; there was a grand parade of troops, with military mass by the Bishop, and a great ball given by the Governor in the evening. Manila is a very pleasant place, and, although my stay there was longer than I anticipated, Mr. T——, by his kindness and attention, made my visit very pleasant, and I enjoyed myself very much. I have sent home my Japanese goods by Twing's barque D. Godfrey, from Hong Kong, and have sent other small packages by other conveyances,—and by Captain Waters, some views of places in the Island of Susan, and the stem of a very beautiful cactus, in tin with moist grass—the case is air tight

8

and a like package has been sent to Germany with success. I have never seen so fine a flower of the cactus, except the Night-blooming Cereus, which it equals in size.

AUG. 4.—We find we may stay here ten days before we sail for Batavia; the hotel is good, kept by a Frenchman. Our passage here has been very fortunate, as this is the stormy season and we have had only a few hours blow since leaving China; the ship is large and comfortable, with accommodations for forty passengers, and we had only fifteen.

AUG. 13.—Since the last mail, we have been to the opposite side of the island, where the Government have two bungalows, in one of which we lived. It was beautifully situated on the top of a hill, the jungle very thick on one side and a fine sea view on the other. The trees were very tall; I should think some of them were fully two hundred feet high. We had hoped for good shooting, but were disappointed, and did not see anything but monkeys and small birds; one monkey was as large as a boy twelve years old.

I write and repeat much written before about finances for fear my other letters may not reach you, and as I find it more advantageous to negotiate a draft here and take sovereigns to Java. We leave in the morning, at daylight, by mail packet, and expect to return here in a month to take steamer direct to Calcutta. The charge for passage to Batavia and back is one hundred and fifty dollars; as it only takes six days, it is at least enough to secure the company from loss. By the papers I see that they are making great lions of the Japanese in New York; the great ball must have astonished them.

The merchants here live in the country, which is very pretty; the roads are good, and the ride of four miles quite pleasant. Chinese abound here, as they seem to everywhere in the East; in this island they outnumber the Malays. A few days ago, an enormous tiger was taken in a trap, three miles out of the city; he was a very different animal from what one sees at home. Fruit is plentiful; we drink the milk of the fresh cocoanut before breakfast; the pineapples, mangustines and several other kinds are very fine.

LETTER FROM PENANG.

PENANG, OCT. 23, 1860.

We had a long passage from Singapore to this place; the wind was constantly against us, with remarkably fine weather. I shall go to Calcutta in the steamer which leaves in a few days. I write a short letter, as my last was very long, giving an account of our visit at Java, of what places visited, and interesting objects seen there.

This is one of the prettiest places I have ever seen, and a pleasant residence for a short time, but must be dull after the novelty of the situation has passed. Nutmegs grow here in abundance, and the tree is a fine one.

The letter referred to above was never received. We were sorry for the loss, as it contained the account of the voyage to Java, and of his visit at the island; also, a description of a wild-boar hunt in the mountains, in which the animal was shot by

Pickering, but not at first killed. He had a guard of natives, armed with spears, to assist in killing, and for defence, should such an accident happen. When they saw the beast turn to the attack, they ran, leaving him to defend himself; he gave a second charge into his head, without disabling him, and then followed this up with blows from the but-end of the gun, which the boar seized in his mouth, grasping with it Pickering's fingers. He was not much hurt, but it was considered unsafe for him to go to the heat of the seashore, and he had to remain in the mountains until the hand was healed. This he regretted, as his friends had to leave and go by the steamer to Calcutta.

LETTER FROM CALCUTTA.

CALCUTTA, Nov. 8, 1860.

I arrived here a week ago from Penang, and, before landing, received a note from Mr. W——, inviting me to his house. I am now with him, and having a fine time; we have been living in the country, but yesterday moved in. I was much disappointed in the date of my letters, expecting more recent ones. I have written to London to have my letter of credit, and all my letters, sent to the care of the United States Consul at Malta. I shall not go to Constantinople, but direct to Paris, and to Italy at Carnival. I see C—— F—— often, and receive much late Salem news from his letters. Calcutta is very pleasant now, and no climate could be better than this at the present season, and it is now very healthy; the cholera has raged, and the season just passed has been one of the very worst. We ride every morning at six. I expect to start for up country in two days with three of the passengers by steamer from Penang, —Mr. and Mrs. Melbourne, residents of Batavia and former acquaintances at that place, and Mr. Charles Dickens, Jr., a son of the celebrated Mr. Dickens. My friends resident here advise this journey, as the Indian cities are well worth seeing. We go to Rannegunge by rail—it is one hundred and twenty miles from here; we shall then take horse dornk and go to Benares, Delhi, Cawnpore, Lucknow and Agra; from thence to Bombay, where we expect to arrive the ninth of December. We have written to engage our passages by the mail leaving there the twelfth; this should bring us to Marseilles about the seventh of January.

LETTERS FROM PARIS.

PARIS, 15TH JANUARY, 1861.

I received letters from you at Malta, sent from Constantinople, and the letter of credit. It is very expensive travelling by the overland mail, and in fact, in all the steam or packet vessels in the East Indies. Your last letter received was of October 2.

The day after my last letter, our party started from Calcutta on our up-country journey. At Rannegunge we took horse dornk, as it is called, for the North. We had very good ghurries; they are so arranged that one sits up or lies

3*

down by changing the seats; we always slept in them
except at large stations where there were hotels; it is a
very comfortable way of travelling, and we all enjoyed the
journey very much. Our first stopping place was Benares,
then Allahabad, Cawnpore, Lucknow, Delhi, and Agra.
Lucknow is the finest city and next comes Delhi. It is
really wonderful how the English took the last place with
so small a force; the fortifications are very strong. The
palace of the King of Oude, at Lucknow, is a wonderful
place, and the gardens must have been perfectly splendid;
it has a pond, with a very handsome bridge crossing it
built of white marble, and there are several pavilions, of the
same material, of very fine workmanship. The Taj, at
Agra, is the finest building in India; it is of the finest white
marble and very splendid; and there are two tombs of the
same. When at Agra, we found that it would take longer
to reach Bombay than we had anticipated, and feared that
it would be very tiresome; so we turned and travelled as
fast as possible for Calcutta, arriving there in time for the
steamer, which sailed early the next morning.

We had only thirty-five passengers to Galle, Ceylon; here
we found as many more, from Australia and China. The
steamer was the Malta, a fine vessel of nearly two thousand
tons, very fast and comfortable. We stayed at Galle two
days, which was long enough to see what was worth our
notice; two and a half days at Aden, where I met our
townsman, Mr. J—— W——, who invited me to his home,
where I remained while there; and in Egypt we stopped
two and a half days;—so that I saw much without waiting
a mail. Mr. Dickens, with whom I had roomed on the

other side, left here—he waiting a mail. We now took a small ship, the Valette, of only seven hundred tons, and, after the first day, had rough weather and an uncomfortable passage all the way to Malta.

PARIS, 29TH JANUARY.

The weather has been exceedingly disagreeable most of the time since my arrival. I take a lesson in French every morning and gain rapidly; I have seen many of the wonders of Paris, but have much yet to see. My friends, Mr. and Mrs. Melbourne, with whom I have been so long, left Paris last week for England. The news from the United States looks very blue, and worse and worse every mail. What do your Memphis and Pontotoc letters say?

PARIS, 3D FEBRUARY, 1861.

Last night, I received a letter from you. It had been to London, sent thence to Malta, returned to London, and sent to me here. I think you had best direct my letters to Paris for the next three months, and they can be more easily forwarded to me.

So you never received my letter from Singapore, after my return from Java. It was a very long one, covering six pages of large letter paper. The illness, that you heard of, at Singapore, was probably in Java; I hurt my hand at a hunt in Bandary, otherwise I have not been unwell since leaving California. Letters from the States say that it is the opinion of the merchants of New York that our domestic troubles will be amicably settled. The lost letter

contained a list of all my drafts while in India; so will send
you the list again. I wish mother would send me a list of
things to purchase here, suitable for home presents.

PARIS, 20TH FEBRUARY.

Mr. A. P—— and myself leave to-morrow morning for
the south of France and Italy. We go first to Marseilles, and
probably through Nice to Genoa, Turin, and from Genoa to
Naples by water, as it is not now safe by land. I have read
Minturn's New York to Delhi, and prefer it to any book I
have read on India. I am surprised the cactus did not live,
and hope the D. Godfrey is not lost, as my things could not
be replaced.

I have seen most of Paris; the suburbs I have not,
reserving them for summer. I still hope our national
difficulties will be arranged without disunion. I do not
expect to return home before the last of September.

LETTER FROM NICE.

NICE, 2D MARCH, 1861.

We left Paris the twenty-fifth February for Lyons and
Marseilles, thence to Toulon, visited the navy yard and saw
the celebrated iron-plated ship La Gloire, of which so much
has been said; she does not look like a good sea-boat, so
much iron making her too heavy. From Toulon we went
to Hyeres, ten miles; there we remained two days, and
were much pleased with what we saw; thence we came here.
The weather now is as fine as it can be; the grass is as green

as in June with us at home; the trees are in bloom, so are
the wild flowers and in the gardens I have seen some roses,
and the orange trees are full of fruit and look beautifully.
There are many English people spending the winter here,
but very few Americans.

People here who were in Naples a few weeks ago say that
it is perfectly safe there, and that travellers can get along
well,—the newspapers representing things much worse than
the reality; we expect to be there in ten days and after a
short stop go to Rome. We went by railroad from Marseilles to Toulon, and the train had a narrow escape from
accident; several rocks, weighing tons each, fell on the
track only a few minutes before our arrival at the place;
we were detained four or five hours before they could be
removed, no one was hurt.

LETTER FROM NAPLES.

NAPLES, 20TH MARCH, 1861.

From Nice we went to Genoa by diligence, over one of
the prettiest roads running along by the shore of the Medi-
terranean. We were two days going, and the weather was
delightful. After a short stay at Genoa we took an English
steamer for this city, stopping at Leghorn, which place I
did not recognize, notwithstanding the brig Governor Endi-
cott, with a painting of the port, always hung over my
washstand in my chamber at home. We were fortunate in
having two good days for our sea-passage; it has been very
rough generally this spring, and the boats that left here
recently had to put back.

We are in the fourth story of the Hotel Grand Bretagne, with a fine view of the bay. The weather is windy and only tolerably good. We are very busy, as there is so much to be seen of interest here; two or three days we have devoted to the Museum, where are deposited the articles taken from Pompeii and Herculaneum, one day we went to Pompeii, and last Saturday we ascended Vesuvius. The day was very fine and clear, and the view beautiful; the ascent was much easier than we expected from the description of it in Hillard's and Murray's Italy. Sunday evening we went to Sorento, and from there to Salerno, and Pæstum, where the Greek ruins are more than twenty-four hundred years old; they are in good preservation, and are considered among the finest ruins in Italy. We shall leave in two days for Rome, by land, as it is now perfectly safe,—stopping one day at Gaeta, being at Rome during the ceremonies of holy week. There I hope to find an accumulation of letters, as it is sometime since I have received any.

LETTERS FROM ROME.

Rome, April 2, 1861.

I received yesterday your letters of nineteenth and twenty-sixth February and March fifth; they should have been here before, and in future you had best send all letters to London to be forwarded to me as heretofore; this is the only safe course. We came here by vettura from Naples, stopping at Gaeta, and arrived a week ago; we had trouble in finding rooms, the city is so crowded; we were fortunate in the

weather from Naples. I am glad to learn that the Japanese things have arrived safely, and that you think them
handsome.

We have been present at all the ceremonies of holy week,
and have been fortunate in obtaining good positions. Last
evening the illumination, postponed from Sunday on account
of the weather, took place; it was one of the most beautiful sights I have ever witnessed; the night was calm,
and very fine for the purpose. To-night we expect the
display of fireworks.

I find St. Peter's surpasses all my expectations; it is most
wonderful. We have not done much at sight-seeing in general, as the services of holy week have consumed all our
time; still we have visited some of the galleries of paintings
and part of the Vatican, the Coliseum, and Forum. We
shall no doubt remain here two or three weeks longer; then
we shall go to Florence.

I hope our political troubles may be settled, but to me
they look blue enough; I like Mr. Lincoln's address, and
think it good and sensible, and hope he may be able to do
some good. Write me about the Salem Infantry, and tell
me who are the officers besides Captain Devereux.

ROME, 9TH AND 15TH APRIL.—These letters are
devoted to the churches and galleries, and to the
uncertain and complicated condition of our political
affairs.

LETTER FROM BOLOGNA.

BOLOGNA, APRIL 28, 1861.

We arrived yesterday, from Florence, by the diligence. I leave to-morrow, for Milan; shall stay only a day, as there is but little to see besides the Cathedral; and thence to Venice, for a few days. I have your letters of twenty-seventh March and the second of April, and have seen the late Boston papers. I hope we shall not have war; but if Davis has as many men under arms as the papers state, it will be very difficult to keep them quiet. Their credit is poor enough here, and it will not be an easy matter to raise money for them.

The day before leaving Florence, we joined Mr. Appleton and a party from Boston, who had special permission to visit the palace of Prince Demidoff. This is the only one that I have seen in Europe that equals my idea of what a palace should be. It is probably the finest in Europe: there are twenty-one rooms on the first floor, all of them very splendid. He is a Russian; is the owner of a mine of malachite, and one of the wealthiest men in the world. There are vases, fire places and tables made of it, and so abundant is its use that you would suppose it to be of no more value than marble. We saw also any quantity of gold and silver vases, dinner services, besides lots of precious stones, of all sorts.

LETTER FROM MILAN.

MILAN, APRIL 30.

I had a long day, yesterday, in the cars from seven in the morning until eleven at night. The London papers of the twenty-seventh have just been received, with the news of the taking of Sumter. I cannot understand it; forty hours cannonading, and no one killed on either side; the firing must have been very bad. I suppose the border States will now secede, and, if they do not, they will furnish the South with troops and do us as much injury as if openly against us. If a regular war is to take place, I think it best for me to return home, as I do not wish to be away. Will you write me, as soon as you receive this, and tell me what you think I had best do? If you write immediately, the letter will be in London in five weeks. I am going to Venice to-morrow.

LETTER FROM VIENNA.

VIENNA, MAY 10, 1861.

I have your letter of the twenty-third of April. We cannot get any late American papers here, but the London Times is full of extracts from them; the excitement must be tremendous. I hope the Southerners will not be able to take Washington; should they do so, the effect abroad would be very bad for our cause. I am sorry that the President had not called Congress together sooner, and caused an increase of the regular army; I would a thousand

4

times prefer fifty thousand regulars to double that number of militia; the men have not the least idea of what they will suffer. Our Commissariat department is poor enough. We must hold Baltimore, if we are to keep troops at Washington well supplied. I did not realize how troops lived in time of war, until seeing them before Gaeta, and this was one of the best equipped armies that ever took the field, and we were there too late to see the worst of it. About sixteen men lived in a very small hut, made of mud, in most cases without any windows; they were at times wet, hot, cold, and always nasty. It is dreadful to think how this will kill off our men, if they go through a winter's campaign; and a summer one in Virginia would not be much better. The Southerners, in all these things, would be no better off, but they would have the advantage of being on familiar ground and where the population are all favorable to them. They have good officers, having had military schools, where many young men have received tolerably good education, while we at the north have looked at military men as useless and lazy fellows; and they have been less respected in New England, of late, than in any other part of the civilized world. Still, war cannot be carried on with success without money, and they certainly will find it difficult to maintain an army for any great length of time; and here we have the advantage.   •

I shall probably sail for home in a few weeks, as I see no prospect for peace at present. I feel sad enough, as we have none of the excitement of arming to relieve the depressing influences of the state of affairs. I shall not stay abroad; all the pleasure of travelling has gone. How many men did the Infantry take to Washington? I see that a Massachusetts regiment is at Fortress Monroe. We are very anxious for later news, and expect it by to-day's mail. We were thirty-two hours from Venice to Vienna, and most of the way the snow was several inches deep, the route being on high land.

LETTERS FROM PARIS.

PARIS, MAY 21, 1861.

We arrived here from Berlin last Saturday, and have engaged passages in the Arabia for home. She is the next Boston boat, and sails in a week, so you may expect to see me in a few days after this reaches you. We could not get any later home papers in Germany, and the letters were full of war news. Yours of the thirtieth arrived this morning, after several days' delay in London. We have American news to the eighth, and, as Mr. Lincoln has telegraphed for more troops, I expect to hear of a fight by the next mail. I am very sorry so many of our Southern relatives are secessionists: I do not see how it is possible for any right-minded person to acknowledge the right of a State to secede. I do not see what we can do should we conquer them. With our idea of a government of the people, how are we to hold them against their will? The whole matter is involved in difficulties. One good must come from it, however, as it settles for the States remaining in the Union this question, that they have no right to secede. It is useless now to be looking at the future; our present duty is to give them a good thrashing, and to teach them to hold different opinions of the relative pluck of Northern and Southern men. I am glad the government are so vigorously at work. Butler seems to have done wonders, and this enlisting of men for three and five years is just the right course.

MORNING OF 22D MAY.

Have just received your letter of the sixth. You say that the Infantry number one hundred and twenty. What a large company! I should think most of the army officers have resigned, by the number of names one sees in the papers.

I do not feel so confident as you do as to the position of the States of Kentucky, Missouri and Maryland, and hope they will not be allowed to remain neutral. Should they be thus situated they would supply the South with food and men, and do us more harm than if openly opposed. I do not believe in any half-way at this time. You must be for or against the Government.

He arrived in Salem on the twelfth day of June, 1861. He was very much interested in the military, and was constantly with officers, and young men who were proposing to become such and raise troops for the army. His parents endeavored to dissuade him from doing so, and used every argument in their power to prevent it. He did not meet with any encouragement at the State House, and, as he would not enlist with the refusal

of the consent of his parents, the summer passed
without his doing so. He was absent in Vermont
part of this time, and his letters from there (none of
which, unfortunately, were preserved) expressed the
strongest desire to join the army, coupled with
undoubted feeling that it was his duty to do so.
He conversed more upon this subject with his mother
than to his father, perhaps for the reason that she
would listen more patiently to his arguments. At
last, he was evidently so unhappy at his position
and felt mortified at being unoccupied at home.
using this argument to obtain my consent,—that he
was single, had no business, was in health, and had
some little acquaintance with the military life,—If
such as he did not volunteer, how was the army to
be raised, and kept supplied with men? Finally.
becoming convinced that it was wrong to further
oppose him in his performing what he thought it
was his duty to do, I ceased all opposition, and.
although I never gave my consent by word, he knew
that he had my approval.

October twenty-seventh, 1861, he signed the enlistment papers, and was authorized to recruit thirty
men, for cavalry, to join General Butler's New
England Division. This cavalry was to be under
the command of S. Tyler Read, and was to be called

4*

Mounted Rifle Rangers. He opened a recruiting office in Salem, and at other places, and obtained the men, who went into camp at Lowell as fast as engaged,—he, in the meantime, being engaged in duty in camp, or on recruiting service, in Salem or Boston, or in travelling to look up men suitable for this service, which required picked men, of full stature, and competent to make good horsemen as well as good soldiers.

In November, he was commissioned Second Lieutenant in the Twentieth Regiment Massachusetts Infantry, by Governor Andrew. This was done without his knowledge or his application, and respectfully declined by letter, with the reason given for declining, that he had previously enlisted in the New England Division. During the latter part of December, Lieutenant Pickman, with a detail of ten men of the cavalry, left Boston in a sailing ship, with more than one hundred Government horses, as a supply for the troops in part. With these Lieutenant Pickman and Pickering sent their own horses, private property. The ship encountered a storm in the bay, the first night out, in which all of the horses but ten were killed, and these were so injured as to be of little value.

CAPTAIN READ'S MOUNTED RIFLE RANGERS.

The following is the Roster of commissioned officers of Captain Read's squadron of Mounted Rifled Rangers, attached to Major-General Butler's Grand Division:—

Captain commanding the squadron—

S. TYLER READ, Attleborough, Mass.

Second Captain—

JAMES M. MAGEE, Carlisle Barracks, Penn.

Senior First Lieutenant—

J. E. COWEN, Fairhaven, Mass.

Junior First Lieutenant—

ALBERT G. BOWLES, Roxbury, Mass.

Senior Second Lieutenant—

BENJAMIN PICKMAN, Salem, Mass.

Junior Second Lieutenant—

PICKERING D. ALLEN, Salem, Mass.

Captain Read has been engaged actively in the present war from its very incipiency. He was with the Sixth Regiment in its stormy passage through Baltimore, was temporarily on Ellsworth's Staff as Assistant Surgeon, and was with the lamented and gallant young Colonel when he fell in the Marshall House at Alexandria, subsequently in the battle of Big Bethel, and afterward acted as Provost Marshal on the outposts at Fortress Monroe until he came North to raise in his native State the splendid body of men which he now commands.

Captain Magee is an officer from the regular service, and

was second in command at the burning of the arsenal at
Harper's Ferry.   Lieutenant Cowen was attached to the
corps of Engineers in the New York Eighth Regiment, and
was in the heat of the battle at Bull Run, in which he was
slightly wounded.   The remaining lieutenants of the corps
are men of experience which well adapts them to their
positions.   The squadron has been raised by selection to a
high standard of excellence, enough applications having
been rejected since the opening of its enlistment rolls to fill
a regiment.   They are tall, athletic, vigorous men, of reliable
character, and present the finest appearance of any corps
which has yet left for the war.

Lieutenant Pickman, in charge of a detachment of the
men, with the horses and equipments of the corps, left for
Ship Island several days since.   The remainder of the
squadron will embark on the Constitution for the same
destination.   They carry heavy sabres and short rifles, and
are to be provided with revolvers beside.

Although enlisting in October, he was not sworn
and mustered into the service until the twenty-seventh
day of December, 1861.   The cause of this delay was
that when the United States mustering officer was at
camp in Lowell, for that purpose, he was absent on
recruiting duty, at offices in Boston or Salem, or in
travelling through the State in pursuit of men capa-
ble of performing cavalry duty.   His position was
that of Second Lieutenant of Captain Magee's Company, enough men having been enlisted for two

companies,—and a third company of cavalry had also been enlisted at Lowell.

Neither Pickering, or myself for him, desired a too responsible position. Both of us had seen large armies engaged in war, or about to do so,—had been over battle fields, and had seen enough to teach us how little we actually did know, and were well aware of the want of military education in so large a proportion of the officers of our volunteers. The company left Camp Chase in Lowell, January 2, 1862, for Boston, were inspected on the Common by Major General Butler, embarked the same afternoon on board the steamship Constitution, with Colonel Shepley's Maine Regiment and Colonel French's Massachusetts. The ship went into the stream, and anchored at evening. The night was exceedingly cold and windy; in consequence the men suffered severely. After a few days, steam-pipes were arranged around the hold of the ship and they were made more comfortable. The cold weather continued many days, and the ship remained in the harbor. This detention was very tedious and dispiriting to both officers and men; the more so, as, for military reasons, the cause could not be made known. It was supposed, then, to be a consequence of the controversy between Governor Andrew and Major-

General Butler; but from a recent statement of the latter, it seems that it was caused by the threatening aspect of our relations with European nations, more particularly with England. On the tenth of January, the troops were ordered to land, and Colonel French's regiment commenced to disembark. Three companies had pitched their tents in Fort Independence, when orders were received to sail for Fortress Monroe. This change in the aspect of things put all in high spirits.

EXTRACTS FROM LETTERS AND DIARY.

Pickering then goes on to say in his journal :—

On the thirteenth, the cold still continuing extreme, we sail early in the morning, with a strong northwest wind—the sea not rough for this coast in winter.

We arrive at Fortress Monroe January sixteenth. In the forenoon I went to the Rip Raps, and then on shore to see my friend Merriam; ascertained that he had gone home on furlough. Passed the night with Lieutenant Cartwright, of the old New England Guards, and went on board ship morning of seventeenth.

On Monday, the twentieth, all the men were disembarked and landed on the beach, near the Fortress, for change of air and cleaning of the ship; being in charge of the guard, have had some hard work; the weather was as fine as possible. At dark it rained, with a thunder storm, which lasted all night; the men suffered from wet, as very few of them were well sheltered and many of them not at all.

22D JANUARY.—The storm continues, but the tents are all ready, with the sand very wet.

23D.—The weather is worse; windy, with rain and hail.

24TH.—More stormy than ever, windy and rainy. In the afternoon we are flooded by the tide; strike camp and go to the woods, where we pass the night in our tents,—we and all our things are well soaked.

25TH, MORNING.—It is still raining, with much less wind and a change in its direction; we begin to think it will never clear. It clears at noon, and looks as if it would continue so. Not feeling well, I go on board the ship to consult the Doctor.

A letter—dated on board ship Constitution—of twenty-seventh January, says,—

I have the measles; this, you know, is the second time; we have about one hundred and fifty cases on board, but very little other sickness. Quite a number have the measles the second time; it is slight and does not last more than four or five days, in these instances, when in the full, or fresh subjects, it runs fourteen. This is my third day, and I am almost well. We have only a few cases in our company and I do not expect many more, as all the men are encamped on the beach, below Fortress Monroe, and those having it are on board ship, where they are very comfortable. I expect to be all right in a day or two, and shall be careful not to take cold.

Last week was a tough one; the weather was very bad and we were encamped on the beach. We landed Monday morning—of a splendid day; but before night a severe storm commenced and many of the men were all night without any shelter, although most of the tents were pitched. I was Lieutenant of the guard, and our company were, most of them, detailed for that duty. I quartered, when not on duty, on board a small steamboat. The storm lasted until Saturday noon. Friday evening the tide had become so high, from the wind blowing strong in the same direction such a length of time, that our camp was overflowed, and we had to strike our tents and go to the woods and pitch them there until morning, when the wind changed; and since that afternoon the weather has been fine.

Merriam is stationed about a mile from the Fortress, at Camp Hamilton, where there are two or three regiments. A New York regiment in the Fortress and other regiments near here drill remarkably well, and are under good discipline. The news from Kentucky is cheering, and I hope we shall soon hear of another battle, on a larger scale, with similar result. The fortifications on the Rip Raps are to be very powerful, but much smaller than Fortress Monroe. The United States sloop Pensacola sails to-day for Ship Island, and we hope to do so sometime this week. Pickman must be melancholy there, but he will find plenty of work if he and the ten men still have charge of a hundred and fifty horses. I have not yet received any letter from you, but hope to soon. Suppose you are waiting for me to give directions how to send.

CAMP HAMILTON, FEBRUARY 1.

Your letter, with a Salem Gazette, has just arrived. I am well again, and came on shore yesterday. As it was rainy, came out here and passed the night with Merriam; as the rain continues, shall stay until to-morrow morning. I have just returned from our camp, where I went on Merriam's horse; it is about three miles from here, and the road leading there is muddy enough. Our men are very comfortable; every tent has a fire in it, and plenty of wood is furnished. The measles are subsiding, the number of cases diminishing rapidly; but a few cases in the Massachusetts regiments. Merriam has fine quarters,—the lower part of wood and the upper of canvas, and as comfortable as possible. We are now waiting for a fair day to embark, as Colonel Shepley arrived from Washington, on the thirtieth of January, with sailing orders. We are going to Ship Island. The first Salem papers received gave me the news of C—— P——'s release. We get all our news from the New York papers, with occasional rumors here, which most always prove false. Last Sunday we could see the secession flag, flying over their works the other side of Sewall's Point, plainly enough to distinguish the colors; it has not been up since. This camp is quite large; there are three or four regiments, besides the Massachusetts Sixteenth, and one of cavalry, of twelve hundred men, from Pennsylvania. A very fine band, attached to the New York Twentieth, is next to this. I saw W—— this morning, he is very well; if he is in want of anything, will see that he has a supply. Officers

5

and others are continually coming in the tent and going, so
you must expect a remarkable letter. The Constitution has
changed her position, nearer the wharf, and has taken in
fresh provisions and a new stock of coal, and is ready for
sea. We received several days since, from Head-Quarters
of the Army at Washington, an order appointing us to act
as officers of the First, Second and Third Companies of
Cavalry of the New England Division, to be attached to
Colonel French's Regiment while dismounted, and stating
that the commissions would date from the time we were
mustered into the United States service.

SUNDAY, FEBRUARY 2.—This is a fine day, and the
men are going on board ship. We shall probably sail
to-morrow.

SHIP ISLAND, 13TH FEBRUARY.

We arrived yesterday, and landed immediately. Our
camp is on the right; pitching our tents and other work
gave us a fatiguing day. We left Fortress Monroe on Tuesday morning, fourth instant, and returned the next day, with
the United States gunboat Miami in tow in distress, a new
boat, built in Philadelphia. We did not sail again until next
day, so that we felt quite discouraged at the repeated delays.
We have had perfect weather since. The voyage was a
splendid one; the health of the men improved, and we have
now scarcely any sickness, with the exception of a few cases
of pneumonia, some of these quite serious on the measles
patients, from exposure after convalescence. The measles
have almost disappeared. I am perfectly well, so is W——.

Lieutenant Pickman and men arrived safely; they lost all the horses but five, out of one hundred and fifty odd. Our own fine horses died. Will you purchase and send me half a dozen pairs of blue goggles by the first opportunity. To-day two or three secesh gunboats made their appearance, some of ours chased them. They fired at each other at the longest range, without doing any damage. So many horses have been lost, we may have to wait several days longer for others on the way before mounting the men. At this time there are not half the required number here. The island is not so gloomy a place as I expected, and, as there are now four infantry regiments and our cavalry and the battery of artillery, it seems quite cheerful. The regiments that came before us have improved much in drill and discipline, and we now hope to do so rapidly. I expect to enjoy the work. I am now to act as adjutant of the battalion, with one of the orderly sergeants as sergeant major. Probably we shall have our horses next week; we do not want them before. It will be uncertain when and how we shall have opportunity to write, but trust it will not be so with you. To-morrow General Phelps will inspect us, and we are to drill before him.

FEBRUARY 18.—The Constitution has been delayed by bad weather and fog. Our camp, on the right, is nearly a mile from the wharf, or fort, or city, as it is called. We are very well; so are most of the men. The weather has been very bad for three or four days. Three of our men, who had been detailed to take charge of baggage on the Constitution, left here in a surf-boat the night of the sixteenth instant, and have not been heard from since. One of them was recently made quarter-master sergeant by Captain Read—he had five letters of recommendation, was a Southerner; the second was an Englishman; the third was Hurter, born in Syria, son of an American Missionary. They may have been blown to sea; probably they have deserted; and it is possible they are stowed away in some ship.

MARCH 5.—A steamer will leave to-night or to-morrow, and I write, although there is very little news here that you have not heard long before. I have seen New Orleans papers of the last. of February. We seem to have gained several important victories. Twelve thousand prisoners, taken in Tennessee, appears to be a small estimate, or three thousand at Roanoke Island. Have heard from the three men who left us, or rather the Constitution; they landed at Mississippi City, and are now in New Orleans. In their account of the troops on the island, they omit the Connecticut Ninth Infantry, and give our number as one hundred and eighteen, when, in reality, the three companies number over two hundred and sixty. We have had very cold weather recently. A party have been on Horn Island the last two days; they brought back ten cattle, and a negro they found there. He had drifted there in a boat, and could not get back to the main land; he was almost starved when he arrived here. The men are healthy and in good spirits. Recently, we had a review of the four regiments, our cavalry, and the Salem Artillery; it passed off finely, although the day was hot; it was intended as a compliment to the new flag-officer, who is to command the gunboat and mortar flotilla proposed to be sent up the river.

The gunboat New London is very active and captures many small craft; one morning she brought in eleven oyster and fishing boats, of twenty or thirty tons; as they were mainly loaded with oysters, we were well supplied for a few days. The South Carolina brought in the Southern steamer Magnolia, loaded with cotton; she is valued at two or three hundred thousand dollars, vessel and cargo.

I am expecting to hear from you soon; have not yet. W—— is well, and wrote home a few days ago. I expected the mail steamer would remain until to-morrow, but now hear she will sail this afternoon, so must close. We have now over two hundred horses, many of them just arrived; they are to be issued to the companies to-morrow, when drilling them will commence; I have a good grey, that I ride daily and expect to purchase. We have been mustered for pay; the men are paid from the date of their enlistment; I shall receive only about one month's pay, as I was mustered in only on the twenty-seventh December and do not get pay for the time in camp and on recruiting service. Several ships are now due, and expected to arrive, with stores and troops. The ship Undaunted lost but four horses of her freight; they were loaded by private parties, who were to pay for all lost on the voyage.

SHIP ISLAND, MARCH 11.

I received a letter from you yesterday. I suppose you will hear great stories of our troops being defeated at Mississippi City, through the Southern papers, before you get the truth of the affair. Last Saturday, Colonel Jones, with

5*

officers and one hundred men, consisting of fifty men from
Company I, of the Twenty-Sixth Massachusetts, and the
same number from Company B, went in the steamer Calhoun to reconnoitre about the place (Mississippi City), with
the view of sending some regiments over there; they found
the wharf or bridge badly broken, but crossed, and found
the houses near the landing deserted; after going a short
distance beyond, they saw two or three horsemen in the
woods, quite a distance from them; soon after, a number
more appeared, when Colonel Jones halted and turned in
the direction of the wharf; the rebels in the woods then
opened fire with some small field pieces, using canister shot.
One of our men was slightly wounded, the merest flesh
wound; this was the only casualty on our side. We did not
fire a shot until on board ship again, when the Calhoun fired
three shells into the woods, with what result we do not
know. There are now seven or eight thousand men on the
island, half of them drilled and disciplined. It would be
easy to hold Mississippi City, with few men, if it were
desirable.

We hear reports of a major coming out to take command
of the cavalry, and of other cavalry companies coming to
join us. Quite a number of the officers here will undoubtedly be ordered home if Governor Andrew has the control
of the commissions. Captain Dudley, of the regular army,
is to command the Massachusetts regiment, and it is now to
be ranked as the Thirtieth. General Butler is expected
to arrive soon, and we to move shortly after. The Navy
are preparing for the attack on New Orleans, and are confident of success.

It is not dull here, ships are arriving every day; six of the mortar fleet have arrived to-day; small prizes are often brought in; a large steamship, now in sight, **may** be the Mississippi. Some of the large ships have to lighten to get over the bar. The United States ships Colorado, Mississippi, Hartford, Richmond, Pensacola and Brooklyn, with a **fleet** of gunboats, are near here, and come in and go out frequently; they are very fine ships. I dined Sunday, **on** board the Richmond, on green turtle and roast chicken,—very different food from our shore fare, which is rather **poor**. We are having **fine weather, and I quite enjoy this mili**tary life.

SHIP ISLAND, MARCH 18.

I have received the letters and papers you sent by Adams' Express, but nothing by the Constitution, which arrived last **week** and sailed again day **before** yesterday. She brought three regiments,—one from Michigan, one from Iowa, and one from Wisconsin; they have been stationed **at** Baltimore and in Virginia, **and** are under **good** drill. Brigadier-General Williams came also; he was on General Scott's Staff, and ranks high **as** an officer of the regular army. We drill six hours daily—two-thirds of the time mounted—and make good progress. There are now on the island, eleven regiments infantry, several batteries artillery, **and** one battalion **of three** companies cavalry; other regiments and batteries are expected daily. I never was in better health; the measles left me rather weak for two or three weeks, but I have now completely regained my strength. I have an excellent servant, a contraband, and as good a man as I could wish; he washes well, and takes good care of my horse, which I care much more about. I do not know when this will go, and leave it at the express office for safe keeping. General Phelps is still in command; he has a New Orleans paper which boasts of advantages gained over our troops, which I do not credit. We have various stories about our movements, and cannot tell what to believe; General Butler is expected to arrive to-morrow.

MARCH 24.—A mail leaves immediately, by a gunboat just arrived from the passes, so write just to say that W—— and myself are well, as you seem to imagine us in a miserable condition. We are as comfortable as possible; no great variety of food for the table; we have rice, nearly all the time, with salt beef and pork, and plenty of bread and butter.

General Butler has arrived, and the troops have been put into brigades. The battalion of cavalry has been divided, and our company has been placed with the Third Brigade, which consists of the Massachusetts Thirtieth, Maine Twelfth, Fourteenth and Fifteenth Regiments Infantry, and the Maine First Battery. Captain Magee commands our company; we are gaining rapidly in drill; I enjoy the mounted exercise very much, and the men have improved in riding. Your letters of fifteenth and eighteenth of last month came a few days since.

SHIP ISLAND, APRIL 2.

Lieutenant Bowles has been appointed Aid-de-Camp to General Shepley. Great preparations are being made for the expedition to New Orleans, and we expect to move in a few days, but I think it will not be for a fortnight. The regular mail will leave in a day or two, and I will try to write; we are quite busy drilling, and have but little time for letters. The Connecticut Ninth left here yesterday, in a steamer, with two gunboats as convoy; we think they have gone to Mississippi City and Pass Christian. The secesh fired on a flag of truce, at Biloxi, the day before yesterday; no one hurt. Have letters from you of twenty-eighth February, and from A—— and L—— and T. Weather clear and warm.

13TH APRIL.—About half the troops have marching orders and will soon leave ; our company does not go, but Captain Read's and the other company do. The attack on the forts will be made this week. We have many mortar boats, several first-class gunboats, and four or five steam sloops of war. The New London took a schooner, yesterday, with a cargo of molasses; she had Mobile papers on board, of sixth April; these mention a battle as then going on, in Tennessee or Mississippi, in which their General Johnson had been killed. It is uncertain when we leave.

13TH, P. M.—I wrote you a few lines this morning, by the mail steamer; she came in last night, and we were not knowing of it, and only had time to get short letters ready and on board with the despatches sent by the General. The night before last we had a fearful thunder storm; I have never seen it lighten so steadily as it did most of the night; the guard tent of the Thirtieth Massachusetts was struck, and three men killed, and two so badly wounded as to be considered hopelessly so, and two wounded slightly. I like my horse much; he stands fire finely; does not mind it the least. We are now at target practice and shoot from our horses daily; they are becoming quite well trained and gain faster than I thought possible. The Connecticut Ninth went to Pass Christian and Mississippi City; at the Pass they captured a camp, equipage, etc., but the men belonging there, a Mississippi regiment of eight hundred men, fled. The Connecticut regiment burned the camp and captured a few men. We have New Orleans papers of late date, and learn by them that the colonel of the regiment was placed under arrest for leaving without fighting. The New London has captured a steamer from Mobile for New Orleans, with thirty-six passengers and cargo of rosin and turpentine.

We expect the attack on the forts will commence to-morrow. We have a powerful fleet and well armed, and in addition, Commodore Porter's mortar fleet. The rebels have a number of gunboats, and are supposed to have about two hundred heavy guns mounted, besides those on Forts Jackson and Phillip; so they are well prepared. It must be a great battle, if we succeed and they defend the forts as we expect they will. Captain Read and his and the other cavalry go dismounted; we remain here, probably two or three weeks longer. The troops are healthy and in good spirits.

Yesterday I received the Salem Gazette, of fourteenth and eighteenth March. Weather very fine. Last week we had a review of the division by General Butler,—about fifteen thousand men. It is a long time, now, since we have received letters from home; the George Washington, with a mail, is expected soon.

SHIP ISLAND, APRIL 19.

The expedition sailed April sixteenth. We suppose they have gone to the forts with the expectation of garrisoning them, when taken by the fleet. You refer in your letter to the overflow in our camp; it was news to me; a high tide may have invaded a small place, with a few tents, but nothing of consequence.

APRIL 25.—We are still here, and, for all I can see, likely to be for some time; we are in readiness to move at any moment. We received news, yesterday, from the Passes; fighting commenced last Thursday afternoon; our dates are up to Monday evening. I have conversed with the captain of the vessel bringing the tidings; the mortar boats are anchored very near the shore, about two miles from Fort Jackson; they are near the woods, and, being covered with boughs and leaves of trees, can hardly be seen from the forts, and they can only judge of their positions from the firing. One of them had been sunk; a ball passed directly through her. The fort had been twice on fire, and an explosion had taken place. All the guns but two appeared to have been silenced; he feels sure that we have taken both forts before this. Several fire rafts have been sent down the river, but without doing the least damage. There is a large chain crossing the river near the forts; naval men think that can easily be disposed of. The rebels appear to have a number of gunboats above the chain, several supposed to be ironclad; they may do us much damage, probably much more than the forts will.

I am yet without a commission; do not see what difference it will make, but should rather have one from Massachusetts. My servant is good, could not have brought from the North a better. I do not think this war will be closed very soon. We are well; go to bed early, and rise at five in the morning.

MAY 4.—I have received many letters, they were very old dates, some early in March. This island is long and sandy, not a single tree for six miles. Four regiments and parts of two others leave here to-day and to-morrow for New Orleans and Fort Pike; we have to remain here still longer. I am now living in a small wooden house some of our men built out of old boards; it has a brick floor, and is very comfortable in pleasant weather, but not so good when it rains; it took three men half a day to build it, so you can imagine how it looks, with three large windows and a door, but no glass in the windows. The Navy have taken New Orleans and gone up river.

SHIP ISLAND, MAY 5.

Of the surrender of New Orleans you will have heard before receiving this. The naval officers and men have done splendidly. The Twenty-Sixth Massachusetts Regiment is garrisoning the forts and the other troops occupy the city. Part of the fleet has gone up the river. The steamer Tennessee arrived here last Friday, in command of an officer of the Richmond; he gave me a very interesting account of the naval operations.

We are very tired of staying here and hope to be ordered somewhere soon. The Maine Thirteenth, Fourteenth and

Fifteenth, the Vermont Seventh, and part of the New Hampshire Eighth, a battery, and our cavalry company, make up the list of troops remaining here now. I think we shall have to remain in this region some considerable time yet, until next spring, if not longer, notwithstanding our success in New Orleans. I want to hear from Virginia very much, and what progress McClellan is making there. We have a newspaper printed here; I send you a copy containing the "glorious news" of the capture of the forts, and that New Orleans is in our possession; it will no doubt be short lived.

MAY 6.—The mortar fleet has returned, and I believe a number of steamers are also coming, so hope that a move is in prospect for us.

MAY 10.—The mail steamer has just come in, and will leave in a few hours. I sent several letters by the Eliza and Ella, a sailing ship, three or four days since; she put back yesterday afternoon in a sinking condition. We expect to go to New Orleans as soon as transports arrive; have not received our orders.

Captain Magee and forty men have been in Biloxi the last two days; they returned last evening; they found very few people over there, and those they did meet were most of them aged. I send you a few New Orleans papers, as specimens of the effect of secession upon them. This steamer will carry three days later news, as she is direct from there. We are anxious for the Northern mail, soon due, for the news, as the rebels in New Orleans have had placards up announcing the defeat of McClellan's army and the occupation of Arlington Heights by their forces. We do not credit these stories, and suppose they circulate them to keep up the spirits of the people.

MAY 19.—Received marching orders, and expect to go on board the ship Ocean Pearl. Sent thirty men on board to put up stalls for the horses.

MAY 20.—Received orders to embark on board the steamer Sallie Robinson, a prize, which arrived here yesterday. Have our horses and everything on board before dark.

21ST MAY.—We sail this morning for New Orleans, by way of Lake Ponchartrain. Arrive at the Orleans Cotton Press at midnight, and find it no easy thing to obtain food for men or horses; finally procure some hay and oats.

NEW ORLEANS, MAY 29.

We arrived here the same night that we left Ship Island, our men and horses in perfect order. We marched from Lake Ponchartrain, and have fine quarters well up town, two or two and a half miles from the Custom House; we have a large hall for the men and a fine stable for the horses, and are in what is considered a healthy part of the city, which is very quiet and appears to be well governed. The Union feeling is quite strong, particularly among the foreigners and the poorer people. I found my friends in the other company well. The weather is fine, though hot; we feel the heat less here than on Ship Island. We are recruiting here, and shall fill the company with excellent men in a short time; quite a number have enlisted in the different regiments since our troops arrived here; a majority of them are foreigners. We have rumors of disasters to our forces at the North, which I hope are not true.

The Constitution and another large steamer arrived yesterday. Commissions came for most of the officers of the Massachusetts troops, but none for P—— and myself; a second lieutenant came to take the place of the second lieutenant of the third company. I felt sure of being commissioned, as Colonel Dudley recommended me and so did Captain Magee, and I cannot understand the proceeding. The Captain has not yet received his papers from the Government; they probably will throw some light upon the subject. If I am not to be commissioned, I shall come home, which I should be sorry to do at present, as the company is well disciplined and drilled, and I should dislike very much to leave it. I can think of no other reason for the Governor's action in refusing me a commission than that I did not accept the one given me in the Twentieth Regiment. Colonel Dudley is now assistant military commander of the city.

MAY 29.—Not well.

MAY 30.—I have typhoid fever; send for Dr. Blake as physician.

JUNE 3.—Have Dr. Hyde, a city physician.

JUNE 7.—Have Dr. Black.

Letters written at Pickering's suggestion, during his illness, were received by us until he had so far recovered as to write himself.

NEW ORLEANS, JUNE 16.

I am now much better, and am up and dressed. The company left here the day before yesterday for Baton Rouge; I do not think they will have any fighting in this vicinity. I expect to be removed down town to the Park Hotel to-day, and shall come home as soon as I get strong enough. I am dreadfully thin, but gaining rapidly; was in bed seventeen days, and for a week very ill. W—— went off in fine spirits. I do not feel inclined to accept any other position after having received such treatment from Governor Andrew.

JUNE 18.—Mustered out of service by Captain Kinsel, Chief of Artillery, of General Butler's Staff, in consequence of a commission from Governor Andrew being sent out to Private Morton, as second lieutenant, to fill my position in the second company of cavalry. I now expect to sail for home to-morrow in the ship Parliament, a sailing vessel; she is not fast, but is large and comfortable. The steamers now going to New York are small and crowded, and they charge a hundred dollars for the passage; I am not strong enough to stand a crowded steamer, and am so thin you would hardly know me. I had quite a conversation with General Butler this morning; he urged my staying here and offered me a position ; I of course declined, as it was necessary for me to first recover my health. The Captain of the Parliament is an old acquaintance, I having dined with him several times at Ship Island; and it was only just now that I heard she was here; I had thought she had sailed long ago; she probably goes to Boston, and should be there about the tenth of July.

JUNE 19.—Went on board ship to sail for home. Sent a remembrance to Dr. Hyde for medical attendance.

ON BOARD SHIP PARLIAMENT, JUNE 20.

Towed by steamer down the river; had to anchor for the night inside the bar.

JUNE 21.—Towed over the bar at 8, A. M.; no wind, and we drift to the westward.

JUNE 28.—We have had very light winds all the week, and are about one hundred and thirty miles from Tortugas.

JUNE 29.—Very hot and calm.

JUNE 30.—Get aground on a bank near the coast of Florida; we get afloat without damage to the ship.

JULY 1.—In sight of Tortugas all day, with the wind off the land.

JULY 3.—Tortugas light house still in sight; we are at last fairly round it, with a head wind and rough sea.

The passage to Boston after this date was pleasant, with the customary changes of calm and rain and fine weather. Pickering arrived home the sixteenth July, with his health much improved by the sea voyage.

On his return home, he heard that a commission as second lieutenant of the first company of cavalry had been sent him to New Orleans, a vacancy having been made in that company by promotion. This

6*

commission he had passed at sea, and his health being
such as to make it doubtful how soon he could return
to duty at the South should he accept, after a short
stay with his family in Salem, he went to the hilly
region of Vermont, by invitation of friends there, to
regain his strength in the pure and invigorating mountain air. The commission arrived safely at company
head quarters at the South. It was returned to him at
Salem, with urgent wishes of the commander that he
would accept; when received here it was forwarded
to Vermont, and received by him at a time of great
excitement in the month of August, when orders for
more troops had just been issued. He soon returned
to Salem, and, upon consultation with military friends
at Boston, accepted the commission, and was mustered into the United States service the second time
on the eighteenth day of August, 1862, as second
lieutenant of Captain Read's company of Massachusetts unattached cavalry, and immediately prepared
to embark again to join his company.

He left Salem on the twenty-eighth of August, for
New York, to sail from there as soon as possible. On
the twenty-ninth, he writes :—

I have secured my passage by the steamer Roanoke, to
sail at noon, tomorow; she is considered a fine ship, is of

eleven hundred tons, with side wheels, and is fast.   There
is no Government ship to sail at an early day for New
Orleans, and I was told it might be one or two weeks, and
possibly longer, before one would go, and that it depended
upon regulations made by the department at Washington.
I saw the Seventh New York Regiment when they arrived
from their second term of three months service; of course
they appeared well.   Two steamers sail from here next
Wednesday for New Orleans, and I shall hope to hear from
you by them.

NEW ORLEANS, 10TH SEPTEMBER, 1862.

I arrived yesterday, and found that Captain Magee had
gone North, very ill; that Lieutenants Batchelder and Morton were at the hospital, with typhoid fever. The city in
general is healthy. I will write on Saturday; have been
extremely busy all day.

CAMP WILLIAMS, SEPTEMBER 12.

I am now with the company.   We are attached to a
brigade under Colonel Dudley, acting as brigadier general;
it consists of the Sixth Michigan, Thirtieth Massachusetts,
Seventh Vermont, First Louisiana, Fourth and Sixth Massachusetts Batteries, and the Maine First Battery and our
cavalry. The Louisiana regiment has about nine hundred
and fifty men, and appears well. The Second is nearly full,
and is commanded by Colonel Paine, who was major in the
Thirtieth Massachusetts when under Colonel French. We
have a pleasant camp, and the company is in good condition.
I saw W—— yesterday; he is thin, is improving, and will

soon be as well as ever. Lieutenant B—— had him taken to the Hospital Hotel Dieu, where he was well cared for; he will be able to join the company in a few days; his fever, like Lieutenant Batchelder's, was caused by exposure and hard work at Baton Rouge.

Think of Lieutenant Batchelder's death. When I landed, I was told that Captain Magee had gone home, and that Lieutenants Batchelder and Morton were at St. James' Hospital, both with typhoid fever. I went to the hospital immediately; Batchelder appeared glad to see me, but he was wandering, and I do not think he knew me. He died the next morning.

The passage out was good,—eight days and some hours. We had pleasant passengers in the Roanoke: Major Strong, Chief of General Butler's Staff, Colonel Weiss and two lieutenants, Mr. Dexter of Boston, and many others. I do not think the rebel troops are very near, although we hear rumors of them often. About two thousand cattle were captured near here last week, and a body of Texan mounted men were attacked and defeated, thirty miles north, a few days since; we captured nearly two hundred horses and quite a number of men without loss to our troops.

Lieutenant Weitzel, Chief of Engineers on General Butler's Staff, has just been commissioned Brigadier General, and I hear is to act Major General, so will be next in command. He is a very able man, was one of the first in his class at West Point, and is now very young, only twenty-six or seven. I want very much to be on his staff and think I may, as it is known that he has thought of me. I should prefer this to any other position; many officers are wanting the place, as he is of the regular army and very popular. I am glad that I returned here, as this division is still my choice; we are enjoying hot, fine weather; this place is about six miles from New Orleans.

CAMP WILLIAMS, 18TH SEPTEMBER, 1862.

Since my last letter, I have received yours, one from T——, and the Salem papers. Did you hear G—— W—— speak? I am glad he is doing well, recruiting for his company, and have no doubt of his success. You do not mention C——; is he going with him? It has rained hard here the last two days, which makes it rather disagreeable in camp. The Northern news seems to be about as bad as possible. General Weitzel's Staff has not yet been announced; it will be when he receives his papers; my chance is good, Major Strong gives me his influence. I have been on quite an expedition; Major Strong started from the city with several companies, one from Connecticut, three from Twelfth Maine, and one from the Twenty Sixth Massachusetts; Lieutenant Morton of General Butler's Staff, Lieutenant Finegross and myself went with him, as aids; we took steamers at Lakeport and went to the other side of Lake Ponchartrain, to the Tarigiparioa river, but could not get far enough up to accomplish anything. We remained Sunday at Fort Pike, went that night to the river near Pass Manchae, at daylight went up with one boat and four companies to Manchae Railroad bridge. The Connecticut company were on the New London, and could not get over the bar. We wanted to get to Ponchatoula, Jeff

Thompson's head quarters, where we heard there were but two companies of militia. One of the Maine companies was sent in the opposite direction to burn a railroad bridge and the Massachusetts company left on board the boat. We had one gun with us, but could not land it, as we had to march nearly two miles on a bridge, stepping from sleeper to sleeper. Our two companies were C and F of the Twelfth Maine, and numbered about one hundred and twenty-five men. There was a locomotive on the track about half way to the town, which of course gave them information of our coming.

On our arrival near the village, they commenced firing with two or three pieces of artillery, and we ascertained from letters and from the negroes that they had three companies of the Tenth Arkansas Regiment and a company of artillery, besides the two small militia companies. After a fight of about twenty minutes we took the town, burned a freight train of twenty or more cars, seized everything in the fort and telegraph offices. I took the telegraph despatches, of which there were several hundred; I enclose one from Jeff Thompson, just received and not delivered, who, it seems, had gone to Jackson the day before. We took his head quarters, and his sword with the inscription " Presented to Gen'l M. Jeff. Thompson by the Patriots of Memphis." Part of our wounded were sent into a house, with a surgeon; the negroes now told us that the rebels were moving in an effort to cut off our retreat, so we moved down the railroad a short distance to await their attack (after we took the village they disappeared altogether), but instead of appearing there, they returned to the village again and seized our wounded. They came back by some road not known to us; they outnumbered us much, at least three to one, and with several pieces of artillery; at this moment, a train of cars arrived, bringing them more men and guns,—probably they were from Camp Moore, thirteen miles above the town; they then commenced a fire of shell and round shot from several pieces, they fired badly and we had but one man wounded.

We had torn up the track, so that they could not follow us with guns on the railroad. We lost three or four killed, and about twenty wounded, of our small number; Captain Thornton of Connecticut, wounded, was taken prisoner when they returned to the village; his second lieutenant was wounded in the foot, but was not taken. When a mile from the town we were joined by the Massachusetts company, which had been sent for, and when five miles further on, by the other Maine company. The rebels followed a few miles, but did not come near enough for the shot to reach us after they left the town; we kept moving slowly and then stopping for them, but they stopped whenever we did. In the skirmish the Maine companies behaved admirably; not a man faltered, and we had no idea of contending with artillery. We had a march of twenty miles on the day of the fight, ten from the bridge to the town, and the weather was very hot.

There is no news here of importance; we expect to be very quiet for some time unless we are attacked, which does not seem probable, as it would require a large force to have any chance of success. The defences of the city are being daily strengthened.

CAMP WILLIAMS, SEPTEMBER 24.

Your letters of the ninth were received yesterday. The weather here now is changeable from cool to very hot. and the reverse. Our New York dates are to the eleventh instant. Are you getting ready to defend Salem? The Salem Gazette and the Boston Saturday Evening Gazette always interest me; please continue to send them regularly. The Army news is discouraging from the North, but we must eventually have the advantage.

This State appears to be full of rebel troops, probably militia in the main. I think Breckinridge, Van Dorn and Jeff Thompson are still in this vicinity, and probably General Ruggles. I trust this winter will finish the war; it is very dull and stupid here with nothing doing; I think I should prefer farming to this, although I am better contented than a majority. General Sherman now commands at Carrollton. and Generals Arnold and Weitzel of the regular army here. or are to have commands here. I do not think we shall be attacked, and feel confident the rebels will be badly whipped if they make the assault.

Dr. Black is here as surgeon of the First Louisiana Regiment, and I frequently see him. There is no yellow fever here, and but little typhoid; chills are very prevalent, and this is the worst month for them. I saw W——, Sunday; he is improving. Five men arrived two days since from our Ponchatoula affair; they became exhausted on the march to the boat and could not get to her in time, and managed to arrive here by land after four days travel; this reduces our loss to less **than** thirty. **This** place is **preferable to** Ship Island; two Maine companies **are yet there. Tell M——** and L—— to write me. If **you see W—— ask him to write and** tell me all about his **company.**

NEW ORLEANS, 29TH SEPTEMBER.

I have just heard that a mail will leave to-morrow, **early,** and have only time to write a few lines at the Post Office to **say** that I have been appointed **First Lieutenant and Aid-** de-Camp on General Weitzel's Staff, **and that I am now on** duty in **my new position.** J. B. **Hubbard,** of the First Maine Battery, is **Adjutant** General and Chief of Staff, with rank of captain; my position is next; and Lieutenant E. E. **Graves, of the** Thirteenth Connecticut Regiment, is Junior **Aid.** The brigade is composed of the First Louisiana, Twelfth and Thirteenth Connecticut, Seventh Vermont and Seventy-Fifth New **York regiments,** two batteries and four companies of cavalry. We go into camp a few miles **from** town this week; the men **are** healthy, excepting **the fever** and ague cases. **W——** has joined his company and **is on** duty again; he has grown stout. I am well as possible, and very much **pleased** at my appointment on the staff.

NEW ORLEANS, OCTOBER 1.

Yesterday I received your letters of September 12; the day before, one of the fifteenth; the papers arrive regularly; G—— W——'s letter has not arrived. The mail which was to have gone early yesterday morning has been detained

7

until this afternoon; so you will probably receive two letters
at the same time.

Speculators have not been making any money by their
operations recently. They have paid high rates of freight;
$60 per ton for hay, and in this ratio for other goods by
steamer. Flour sells for $5 to $8 per barrel; sugar 9 to 10
cents per pound; corn 70 cents per bushel, and oats 65 to 75
cents; hay $42 per ton. They must store their goods, and
they will have to wait awhile before selling, with a good
prospect of a heavy loss.

The weather this week is very fine; a great change from
that of last; we go to camp to-morrow. I hear that Captain
Batchelder was killed in battle at the North; his parents will
have heard of the death of both their sons at the same time.
You seem to be much troubled about W——; he is all right
again, was very ill, and would have had a hard time had not
Lieutenant Bowles paid him special attention and procured
for him superior care. I will send you, by my next letter,
the rebel account of our skirmish at Ponchatoula; it is
decidedly amusing. Our dates from the North are to the
twenty-first; we are delighted with the news.

CAMP KEARNEY, OCTOBER 6.

We are now in camp at Carrollton, about a mile from the
village, and six from New Orleans; the locality is much
preferable to Camp Williams. The accounts in the Northern
papers regarding us here are amusing. They state that we
are in daily expectation of an attack from the rebels. From
our information, they have no force in this vicinity nearly

equal to ours, and there is no probability of their attempting any such operation at present.

We are having continued fine weather; a great change from that of ten days since. I like my new position very much, even better than I expected. General Weitzel graduated the second in his class, and is at present the youngest brigadier general in the army; he is very tall, over six feet. Captain Hubbard is full six feet, and rather taller than myself. Three papers were received this morning, and I am glad to see that C—— S—— has a commission. The Seventy-Fifth New York Regiment, in this brigade, is one of the best in drill and discipline, really excellent. We have fine quarters, overlooking the camp.

CAMP KEARNEY, OCTOBER 10.

I write a few lines to say that we are well, and have received a number of letters; did not know of this mail in time to say much. The Roanoke is below New Orleans, in quarantine.

OCTOBER 16.—The Roanoke was detained at quarantine a week, as she landed passengers at Havana. My last dates from you are of the twenty-sixth ultimo. The Eighth New Hampshire Regiment is now in our brigade, instead of the Seventh Vermont. The Seventy-Fifth New York Regiment drill and look like regulars, and it is the best volunteer regiment I have seen. The colonel is a West Point officer. The weather now is quite cool and fine. My best horse is a large bay, and a very fine one; my second belongs to the cavalry company, and is a very good one.

NEW ORLEANS, OCTOBER 22.

Captains Magee and Cowan arrived yesterday. We are to start on an expedition to-morrow, and you may not hear from me again for five or six weeks.. We probably shall have chances to write, but of this I am not certain. I saw W—— this morning, and gave him some Salem papers. Have received recently a number of letters; also the photograph and caps, by Captain Magee. Please thank for them.

THIBODEAUX, LA., OCTOBER 28.

We arrived here yesterday. Had quite a fight the day before, in which we were successful, having taken one hundred and fifty prisoners, including ten officers, and one brass gun, a twelve-pounder. Our loss was sixty or seventy in killed and wounded. We have marched all day the last week, and start again to-morrow. The prisoners we took were among the first raised troops in the rebel service, belonging to some of their best regiments, and had distinguished themselves at Shiloh. They were strongly posted, but we outnumbered them. I am well; have no time for anything more now.

NOVEMBER 10.—We have not had any mail for some time; but a few days since, lots of papers and several letters came altogether. T—— writes me that G—— W—— will be major of the regiment to which his company belongs. His letter, if he ever has sent one, has not been received. I was in the city last Monday, and saw W——, he was looking well. **Give my love to M——— and L———**, and tell them that if we remain here a few **days I** will write them. Railway communication is **now open** with the city, and nearly so to Brashear City on Berwick's Bay, in the opposite direction. **We** have now undisputed possession of the district of **La** Fouche, which is considered the finest part of Louisiana. The rebels are now on the other side of the bay, near Franklin. A majority of their men are conscripts, who will not fight, as they have not been in the **service** long enough to be well drilled **or** disciplined, **and are very** much dissatisfied. Their **picket deserted last night and** came over to us.

· We have taken, since landing **at** Donaldsonville, five or **six** hundred prisoners, two-thirds of **them** belonging to the **militia,** which has since been disbanded. You will probably **see** the General's report of the affair at Georgia Landing, near Labadieville. The enemy had the Eighteenth Louisiana and Crescent City regiments, Roylston Battery of four pieces, and a company or two of cavalry, on one side of the bayou. Both of these regiments distinguished **themselves** at the battle of Shiloh, but were small, both not numbering more **than** six hundred men. The Crescent **is the** best Louisiana regiment in the **field. Their** batteries were well **served.** On the other side the bayou they had Colonel Vincent's Louisiana Cavalry, Semmes' Battery, (the one that injured us so much at Baton Rouge) the Thirty-Third Louisiana Infantry, and a few militia. The fighting was nearly all on the **side** where the Crescent and Eighteenth were posted. They had a very strong position in the woods, with a large ditch in front of their line. We drove them

7*

from this position, capturing one of their brass field-pieces, and nearly two hundred prisoners; rather more than one hundred of them belonging to the Crescent Regiment. Among the prisoners we had Captain Roylston and one of the lieutenants of the battery, and eight or ten other officers of the Crescent and Eighteenth Lousiana. We buried Colonel McPhutus of the Crescent, and five or six of their men. These were all the killed we found; they may have taken away others. Some of their badly wounded have since died. We lost eighteen killed, and nearly eighty wounded. Two New Hampshire captains were among the killed.

On the other side the bayou the fight did not amount to much. We there lost a few men. If they lost any they took them away. They retired after their forces on the upper bank of the bayou were defeated. They numbered, in all, but fifteen hundred men. All of our force was not engaged. They destroyed all the bridges. The General had ordered flat-boats towed up from Donaldsonville, so that we had a bridge that artillery could cross over on, in ten minutes after the fight commenced. Had it not been for this they would have done us much injury. We are deficient in cavalry in this department; if we had had more we should have taken the other three guns of Roylston Battery; our infantry could not follow rapidly enough.

We have not had any rain since leaving the city, and the weather has been perfect, quite cool, with a heavy frost nearly every morning. I do not remember in my experience such continued fine weather; the men have slept in the open field every night but one since leaving Camp Kearney at

Carrollton. I have been as well as possible, but we have always had a house for head-quarters, sleeping on the floor. We live on the country, and have plenty of fresh meats. I am quite busy, and find my position all that I anticipated. The brigade is an excellent one, the men healthy and jolly; officers and men have perfect confidence in the General; this is as it should be when success is expected. We hear all sorts of rumors, not very reliable, as to the rebels on the other side the bay; they probably number near three thousand, part of them first-rate troops, the rest conscripts and militia; a thousand of them are the same that fought us the other day; they will not be likely to attack us. General Butler and Staff came up here on Friday and returned the next day.

CAMP STEVENS, LA., NOVEMBER 29.

I write this letter in the hope that it will be in time for the steamer that is to sail this afternoon, and to say that no military event of consequence has transpired since my last. We are still in camp near Thibodeaux, fifty odd miles from New Orleans. The change has come, and we are having rain and otherwise disagreeable weather; the men now have tents and are sheltered. My usual supply of letters were received last week, the letter of credit being in one of them. The shooting near here is good, and we get many snipe and ducks. The weather is improving to-day.

NOVEMBER 28.—Yesterday was Thanksgiving day; the weather was perfect; the men had quite a time and looked finely. The secesh have all left, and gone to the other side of Berwick's Bay. We are sending hundreds of horses and mules to New Orleans, for the regular United States artillery stationed there. We are on horseback half of the day; I enjoy it very much, and now weigh one hundred and seventy-five pounds. If this arrives before my package is sent out, please send the belt to my infantry sword.

DECEMBER 8.—We are still in camp near Thibodeaux, with little to do. I was in the city a few days, lately, and saw W——; he was thinking of making application for a commission in the new Texas regiment of cavalry now being raised; Captain Magee will approve his papers. G. W——'s regiment will not have long to serve when they leave the State; it seems poor policy to raise troops for so short time. We are all anxious to hear from General Banks' expedition; the New York papers are full of the matter. The Southerners have rumors of the defeat of General Burnside. The conscripts are deserting the rebels from Port Hudson, and from the other side of Berwick's Bay; we have a number come in every day; last Sunday Captain Perkins captured two lieutenants. The enclosed photograph of Major Strong please put in my book with the others, for preservation; will send one of the General soon.

NEW ORLEANS, DECEMBER 17, 1862.

I have received two letters this week. General Banks and expedition have arrived, or rather, part of the troops, one brigade has already gone to Baton Rouge; the enemy have very few men there, and there will be no necessity for any fighting. We are not particularly pleased that General Butler should have been superseded. General Banks has men enough to take possession of this country, but the great fight of the Southwest will be at Port Hudson, where there is a large force strongly intrenched, and which place will undoubtedly be reinforced. General Weitzel is in town, and has reported to General Banks; he will endorse **W——**'s applicatioh for a commission in the Texas regiment of cavalry. I have been urged to apply for a majority in it, **but** shall not, much preferring my **present position.** The officers are nearly all selected, and there is but little doubt of its succeeding. **We expect to** be ordered **North** (that is, up the river), as **our** brigade is **in fine order, and, for regiments** that have **been in service for more than a year,** very full, the four numbering twenty-eight hundred men for duty, —**then we have** our artillery and **cavalry, besides the First Louisiana, which** is now at Donaldsonville.

NEW ORLEANS, DECEMBER 22.—I have been **in** town **some days past.** General Weitzel expects to return to Thibodeauxville **to-morrow; if he goes, I shall.** The General has been in consultation with **General Banks.** This city **is** now the most expensive one I have ever been in, **much more** so than Paris or London.

We are now **to be in** General Augur's **division,—the** centre brigade ; ·**we are to leave Thibodeaux this** week **and** march **to** Donaldsonville, **and there embark** for Baton **Rouge,** where most of the new **troops are going.** Magee's companies **have gone, and** I **think W——** went with them; **if he did not,** shall see him to-day. Lieutenant P—— has resigned, **and** his resignation has been accepted; he **goes** home in the ship with General Butler and Staff; they sail to-morrow. Enclosed **is** a photograph taken at Jacobs'.

CAMP STEVENS, DECEMBER 29.

There is not much news. Have received several letters
from you, enclosing those from M—— and L——. I will
send them some rebel stamps soon. We seem to have been
badly whipped in Virginia, as usual. I hope General Butler
will be given a good position; he certainly has done well in
Louisiana. Major Strong has been appointed Brigadier,
but he has gone north with General Butler. General
Weitzel is still in New Orleans, with General Banks. We
move as soon as he returns. Our brigade has been broken
up, in order to scatter the old regiments. The Thirteenth
Connecticut and Eighth New Hampshire, both go out of
this brigade, and green ones are to come in to fill their
places, the One Hundred and Sixtieth New York being one
of the new ones. Everything moves very slowly. We
have now been in this camp two months. The weather has
been rainy, and the roads are very muddy. We cannot
leave here, for want of transportation, as the Thirteenth
Connecticut and Eighth New Hampshire took all we had,
and it must return here from Donaldsonville for our use,
unless we leave all our camp equipage. Did I tell you in
my last that I saw E—— P—— in this city. He was
looking finely, and had been acting commissary of a transport, with a New Hampshire Regiment on board. What do
you think of the European powers recognizing the Confederacy? We have heard that Secretary Seward has resigned.
Who will take his place? We cannot even guess.

JANUARY 8, 1863.—We are still in camp here, and have

been joined by several New York regiments of three years men. I have received my box of clothing, which was in first-rate order; all the things were just what were wanted. I do not know when we shall move from this place; suppose not at present. It cannot be intended we should, or the new regiments would not have been sent here. The paper, with the New Orleans letter about our mess, has also been received; it was not exactly true, however. The fifty was for nearly two months, during which time we paid little or nothing for our meats, which are the principal items of cost in our mess bills. I have been in town with the General nearly all of the last month, and it is a most expensive place, particularly for horse hire. We have no news here to communicate, of any kind. Did you see the poetry in Vanity Fair about Weitzel's four thousand, or his elephant, in Frank Leslie's Budget of Fun for January.

JANUARY 10, 1863.—By General Banks' new order I shall have to give up my horse belonging to Read's company. He is not the best one, but I am sorry to lose this old one, as I am accustomed to him, and he is very tough and reliable, and will stand between two cannon when firing, without minding it. He is not worth the quartermaster's price, and I can buy a suitable one for less. It takes a long while to accustom them to fire. The private secretary of General Banks is T——, a Salem boy that I used to know very well years ago, but had not seen for a long time. He has been living recently in Chicago. We have a superior man for brigade surgeon, Dr. B——, of the Seventy-Fifth New York. His age is between fifty and sixty, and he has had great experience. I now room with him. The Seventy-Fifth, the One Hundred and Fourteenth, and One Hundred and Sixtieth New York regiments are in our brigade. We expect to move soon. The city is full of rumors. Many of these relate to us. They say that we have been whipped by the Confederates several times, they having crossed Berwick's Bay. We have not seen them, and only wish they would try the experiment. I have the promise of a bull dog, to be given me in a few days. How would mother like to have him sent home?

NEW ORLEANS, JANUARY 28, 1863.

I have been in town this week past, and return to camp to-morrow. General Weitzel has been to Baton Rouge with General Banks, and has just returned. Our brigade has been on an expedition to the other side of Berwick's Bay. The troops consisted of the Sixth Michigan, Twenty-First Indiana, Seventy-Fifth and One Hundred and Sixtieth New York, Eighth Vermont, and Twelfth Connecticut infantry regiments, the Sixth Massachusetts Battery, First Maine, and Company A, First Regular Artillery, with one Section of Manning's Battery. We started with four days' provisions, and were gone only three days from Brashear City. The object of the excursion was the destruction of the partially iron clad boat, I. E. Cotton.. The rebel force was not more than half so large as ours. We drove them several miles, when they burned the boat. We had quite a heavy artillery fight all day, the enemy having two thirty-two pound guns on the boat, one forty-eight, and two or three twelve-pound howitzers, besides ten field pieces on shore. We had **four** gunboats under Lieutenant-Commander Buchanan, who was killed, and the force named above, under General Weitzel. Our loss was forty or fifty, most of them wounded only, and in the gunboats a dozen more. They could only proceed a few miles above Pattersonville, owing to obstructions in the Teche, where we fished out three large torpedoes, intended to blow up the boats. Our success was complete. The enemy lost many more than we did. We buried twelve of their **dead, and** took fifty prisoners; and at one time **not a man was to be** seen on the deck **of the Cotton, our sharp-shooters driving** them from their guns, or **shooting all that** appeared; the loss on her must have been very heavy. It is expected that our brigade will move again directly. The Salem Infantry are at Carrollton.

THIBODEAUX, JANUARY 30.

I have been two days at Brashear City, on Berwick's **Bay,** this week. **The** cavalry of the enemy are seen from there nearly every day. **It** is now more **than** three **months since** we came here, expecting, at the time, to stop only one night. My pay, including extra staff allowance, is less than it was as lieutenant of cavalry; and as I have **servant** to pay and furnish with **clothing,** and half-pay of the hostler, which expense **Lieutenant** Graves and myself share, my funds do not supply **my wants. The English government pay** their troops east of Suez double the usual home sum, **making the** difference in pay according to cost and station. Our troops should be paid on **a like plan.** When on Ship Island we

8

could not expend half the sum paid us; but at New Orleans and in this vicinity, when we draw our extra supplies from that city, the pay does not meet our expenses. As I do not see any necessity, at least for the present, for any other course, I shall continue to live as I have been accustomed to, and economize when it becomes necessary, and shall draw for what money may be required. The rebels, according to their official report of our last encounter with them, lost one hundred and fifty in killed and wounded. Among the killed the lieutenant-colonel of their cavalry, and Lieutenant Stevens of their navy, the officer who commanded the celebrated ram Arkansas. He commanded the Cotton after her Captain (Fuller) was wounded. Our loss was less; only six killed and twenty-eight wounded; one of the killed being Lieutenant —— of the Seventy-Fifth New York, of the brigade troops. Our boats lost Lieutenant Commander Buchanan and three men killed and eight wounded. We all feel very badly at the loss of Lieutenant Commander Buchanan; he was one of the most able naval officers here, and a very pleasant companion. In the rebels' report they exaggerate our loss, and state it to exceed their own. Lieutenant Commander Cooke now commands our boats. The newspapers we found the other side of Berwick's Bay were printed on wall, or house paper, and of course only on one side.

THIBODEAUX, FEBRUARY 6, 1863.

When in town last week I went to Carrollton. The Infantry are in camp there. I found D—— P—— in the hospital. He was so much improved that he expected to go to Baton Rouge, with his regiment, the next day. I saw W—— and C——, S—— and L——, the evening that I arrived in town. They went to Baton Rouge the next day. W—— had not shaved since he left home, so he was looking rough, but well. I received long letters from you yesterday. The enclosed one, for Mobile, can probably be sent through the lines, ere long. You say that I have been commissioned as first lieutenant of Captain Read's company of cavalry. I am glad to hear of this, although I may never be with the company. I do not have a commission on the staff, only an appointment from head-quarters. The acting Adjutant General is not so situated. In case the General should resign, or give up his command, by cause of accident, or from any other reason, I should be discharged also, unless I held a commission elsewhere. I find my position, on the staff, all that I anticipated, and the General is esteemed as one of the very best officers; and thus far he has succeeded admirably in everything that he has attempted. We expect to move *somewhere* very soon. My newspapers did not come with my letters. They were not ready. I expect to receive them to-morrow.

THIBODEAUX, FEBRUARY 18, 1863.

I received a long letter from you yesterday, and was delighted to get it, as it was quite a long time since I had heard. Half the brigade are still here, and the other half are at Brashear City. The weather has been bad recently, and the mud is horrible. I have been at the bay most of the time recently; went over with twenty men of the Seventy-Fifth New York, and caught two rebel cavalry men, with their horses and rifles. We laid nearly all one rainy night in the mud to do it. It was their outer picket post of three men; the third escaped, we being on foot, and they mounted. I have been in one of the gunboats, all up through the lakes, and several of the bayous; the object being to obtain information, &c. I received a splendid present yesterday of a pair of solid silver spurs from —— of Louisiana.

BRASHEAR CITY, MARCH 6, 1863.

I have received three long letters in the last ten days, during which time I have not written, having been quite busy. The brigade is now called the second of the First Division, and is under command of Major-General Augur. Colonel Dudley commands one of the other brigades, and he is at Baton Rouge. We like our camp here, as we were well tired of Thibodeaux. The rebel pickets are in sight every day, on the other side of the bay, it being about one-third of a mile from the point where we have just built a strong battery, and have already mounted several heavy guns. General Sibley now commands the rebels opposite us. There are two or three of his regiments at Camp Bisland, about ten miles from here, and others higher up. Our brigade is in splendid order, particularly four of the regiments, and they are generally healthy and jolly. One of the new ones, the One Hundred and Sixtieth New York, has considerable sickness; a necessary experience, as it seems, for all new men to suffer. You must congratulate H—— F—— for me; shall write him if I find time. I have seen General Dwight, Howard, and Charles and Fletcher Abbott, and two other Bostonians. General Dwight is at Baton Rouge; General Andrews at Carrollton.

I only hear of W—— through your letters since the company left New Orleans. Have you seen the plan for making the Atchafalaya the outlet of the Mississippi, as published in the New York papers. The mouth of the river is directly opposite this point. I see by the Boston Gazette that the First Battalion of the Second Cavalry have left Massachusetts under Caspar Crowninshield.

The winter has disappeared very quickly, and we seem to be as far from peace as ever, and to have accomplished but little, if anything. I hope in the spring campaign we shall be more successful. General Shepley and Lieutenant Bowles have been here some days, and have just left for the city. I do not expect any fighting before we move, as the rebels will not attack us.

NEW ORLEANS, MARCH 14, 1863.

I came in with the General day before yesterday, and return to camp to-morrow at Brashear. This is a pleasant place, and esteemed as healthy. We are all well pleased with the conscript law, and think it will work advantageously for our army. Men under short enlistments are very much inclined to be counting the time when they are to be discharged, and do not make as good soldiers; and when they

8*

have become hardened to camp life, and learned somewhat of drill and discipline, they are mustered out of service. It is not so with the men enlisted for a long time, or for the war. They do not give it a thought, and consequently are more contented and interested. They have their jokes upon the short-time men, calling them the four hundred dollar men, in consequence of the high bounties that have been lately paid at the north. The rebels in New Orleans are full of rumors relative to our brigade, and many of them believe that we have been badly beaten, and half of us taken prisoners, and the rest driven away. The sole foundation for this story was the firing of a few shots by some Texan cavalry, early in the week. We fired one shell at them, when they disappeared; there was no one hurt. We have such performances every week, and they probably are the origin of the stories which are so common in New Orleans. I have received my commission as First Lieutenant of the First Unattached Company of Cavalry from Massachusetts. It is dated the first day of January, 1863. It came to hand several weeks since. The photograph sent was taken in New Orleans. The group consists of General Weitzel, Captain Alden of the Richmond, Captain Perkins, Lieutenant Terry of the Richmond, Colonel Merritt, Seventy-Fifth New York, and three of Major-General Augur's Staff and others, myself included. You can tell the General by his star.

BAYOU BŒUF, LA., MARCH 24, 1863.

I received several letters and papers by the mail before the last. You fear my having the rheumatism. I have never been so exposed to it as the last four or five months, and have never had so little; one slight touch, several weeks since, one morning, is all that I have had since leaving home last August, and my health could not be improved. I have been up two nights of the last three. Night before last was on the lakes with a gunboat, as a few secesh were there in boats, probably trying to ascertain our whereabouts, as we moved the night before that to this point, seven miles from Berwick's Bay, and near New Orleans. We shall probably return to the Bay again soon. The Confederate ram Queen of the West, and gunboats Hart and Webb are supposed to be in this vicinity. We still hold Brashear with a strong picket, and changed to this place on account of its strength of position. We had quite a lively skirmish, two or three days since, with the secesh picket; they attempted to capture a dozen of our men, when the General sent me over with seventy or eighty infantry. We drove them about two miles, and fired a good many shots, without any one being hurt. They numbered fifteen or twenty mounted men, and kept at very long range. After we had driven them beyond a point the General sent Perkins over with his cavalry. He drove them seven miles, as far as Patterson, capturing five men and six horses, and wounding one other man and several horses. Perkins' horse was shot through the head, and he lost four other horses, but no men. He was then driven back by two or three hundred secesh cavalry, but without losing a man or horse; so this was quite a success for him.

General Banks and several of his staff were here yesterday. It poured nearly all day, so they saw little of the camp. We were all wet enough, and had been for twenty-four hours. They went to Brashear and dined with us, on beans and hard bread and the like. We live pretty well, except when moving, then we are glad to get anything. What do you think of Port Hudson? The troops have all returned to Baton Rouge. The Hartford and Albatross are said to be near the mouth of the Red River. I send you some secesh newspapers, given me near Pattersonville, where I went two days since with a flag of truce. We have been so busy lately, moving and doing one thing and another, that I have not had any time to write. This is a perfect day, and we have our tents up and everything hung out to dry. We all hope to advance soon, and why every thing moves so slowly we cannot tell. Our brigade is in perfect order, and is much praised by all who visit us; and it is the only one that has done anything in this department since its formation last September. General Arnold was also here yesterday. He has just been appointed a brigadier—is a captain in the Regular United States artillery. Have you seen that Major Strong has been made a brigadier? Please send my watch, first having it put in perfect order; my hunter is out of order, the mainspring broken, and otherwise injured. Send by Adams & Co.

April fourteenth, letters were received from General Weitzel and others, giving an account of the capture of the gunboat Diana, with Pickering on board of her, and of his having been wounded and taken prisoner. These letters and newspapers sent us give all the circumstances and particulars of the fight, and the reason for his having been on board the boat.

General Weitzel's letter was dated " Head-quarters Second Brigade, First Division, April 2, 1866," and reads as follows :—

DEAR SIR,—I regret to inform you that your son Pickering, my aid, was wounded and taken prisoner by the rebels, on last Saturday. His wound is not dangerous. The ball passed under his left shoulder blade through his body, and lodged under the skin of his left arm; it has been extracted by my surgeon, who went up under a flag of truce. Pickering is at the house of a surgeon in Pattersonville, and is very kindly treated. He is attended by a number of ladies. We are permitted to send him anything we desire. I sent him up money, clothes, medicines, flour, coffee, &c. He is treated better than the other officers, because, as the rebels say, he behaved in a most brave manner. The disaster is the result of disobedience of orders on the part of the navy officer commanding the vessel. Fearing that this officer was inclined to be rash, I sent Pickering with him, to see that my orders were not exceeded; but although he (Pickering) expostulated with the captain four times, he persisted in disobeying my instructions. I hope that the rules on the non-exchange of officers will soon be rescinded, so that Pickering may soon again join my military family. I can assure you I miss him very, very much. His energy, bravery and good judgment (qualities which I thought I recognized in him, and which caused me to place him on my staff) make him invaluable to me. It may solace the grief of your family to know that, on this occasion, as on a half dozen previous ones, Pickering behaved in the bravest and most gallant manner. At one time he was the only soul fighting the enemy, and he did all he could to prevent the boat from falling into their hands. Hoping that it may never again be my duty to send you such disagreeable news as the above, and with my compliments to yourself and family,

I remain truly yours,

G. WEITZEL,

Brigadier-General United States Volunteers.

Extract from a letter written by an old school-mate, dated "Head-quarters Department of the Gulf, New Orleans, March 31, 1863":—

Your son, Lieutenant Allen, was wounded and taken prisoner, while making a reconnoissance upon the gunboat Diana in Grand Lake. The whole thing was the result of an unaccountable disobedience of orders upon the part of the captain of the gunboat, who was killed at the first fire. He was ordered by General Weitzel to come back by the same route he took on his way up. In fact, to prevent any such thing occurring, your son was sent by General Weitzel upon the reconnoissance. He however persisted in disobeying the orders given him, and against the repeated remonstrances of Lieutenant Allen. The consequence was the capture of the boat, and the killing or taking prisoners of the officers and men. The details you will find in The Era newspaper, which I enclose.

General Weitzel informs me that the ball has been extracted by one of our surgeons, sent up by a flag of truce. He has also communicated with your son twice by flag of truce, since the affair, and has sent him everything he needed. The ball, which General Weitzel gave me, I send you by express. I take the liberty of writing you, as Pickering was an old school-fellow and Salem boy with me.

Yours, respectfully,

J—— F. T——,

Private Secretary to Major-General Banks.

Letter from Pickering, when a prisoner, dated "Pattersonville, La., April 6, 1863":—

You will have heard, before receiving this, of my having been wounded and taken prisoner. I am getting well quite rapidly; have excellent care, and have been treated with the greatest kindness since my capture. I am wounded in the shoulder and arm, and have a cut on the hand, from a fragment of a shell. Dr. Benedict (our brigade surgeon) came by flag of truce to see me, the day after our capture, and extracted the ball. There is now very little, if any danger from my wounds. It is impossible to tell when we shall be exchanged; may be in two or three months; may be in as many days, although I do not think the last chance worth much. I am now at Dr. Grout's, in this village, and am perfectly comfortable. This letter I expect will go to-morrow by flag of truce. Should anything of interest occur in the meantime, will add to this. Give my love to mother, Marion and Lizzie. It is doubtful if I have an opportunity to write again. Yours, affectionately.

Additional note by Captain Cowen, dated " Camp Reno, April 9, 1863 " :—

I enclose a few lines in your son's letter, which I took from his hand yesterday and brought over on a flag of truce. He wished me to enclose this in his letter, as I had seen him two days after he had written.

He is doing well, and is now able to sit up nearly half of the time. He appeared in excellent spirits, and is very comfortably situated, at Doctor Grout's plantation. We have sent him clothes, and such provisions as he could not procure there and they would allow to come inside their lines. I expect they will move him further away from our lines in a few days, as we shall move to attack the enemy to-morrow. I could not tell him of this, for one of their officers was in the room with us all the time I spent with him. Dr. Whitehead went over with me and dressed his wounds. Our troops are on the move, and I must now close. He did not surrender until escape was utterly impossible, and he began to be faint from his wounds.

Very respectfully,   T. E. Cowens,
                                           Captain and Aid-de-Camp.

Full particulars of the capture of the Federal gunboat Diana were furnished by a special correspondent

of the Boston Traveller, dated " Head-quarters Weitzel's Division, Bivouac at Bayou Bœuf, Monday, March
30, 1863, midnight," as follows :—

On Sunday evening the rotunda of the St. Charles Hotel
was thronged, as usual, with its heterogeneous crowd of
people; but early in the evening, the loyal men and our
officers observed considerable jubilation among the rebels
assembled there, who stood together in knots of half a
dozen or more, whispering some terrible tale. We were
not long in ascertaining the cause of this treasonable
commotion, which proved to be the report that the enemy
had captured the gunboat Diana, with two companies of
infantry, at Bayou Teche. Upon making the proper inqui-
ries of the conductor on the railroad running between
Algiers and Brashear City, we learned that the sad news
was indeed true.

Hurrying over to Algiers, an accident happened to the
ferry-boat plying between New Orleans and Algiers, which
caused me to miss the morning train, the only train depart-
ing for Brashear City. Fortunately, an extra train was
loading with a portion of the Twenty-First Heavy Artillery
Regiment, which was ordered to proceed to Bayou Bœuf,
the head-quarters of General Weitzel. Securing a few
crackers and a loaf of bread, your correspondent jumped
into one of the cattle cars, and in a few hours was wending
slowly on his way to the vicinity of the disaster. The train
reached here, a distance of eighty miles, in nine hours.

To Captain J. B. Hubbard, Aid-de-Camp to General

9

Weitzel, and Assistant Adjutant General of Weitzel's Division, who went up on the steamer Southern Merchant. on Sunday afternoon, with a flag of truce, I am deeply indebted for the following interesting particulars concerning this unhappy event. I am also under lasting obligations to several of General Weitzel's Staff for the hospitalities extended on the trip to their head-quarters.

On Saturday afternoon, the twenty-eighth instant, Captain Peterson of the gunboat Diana, having on board a detachment of twenty-nine men from Company A, Twelfth Connecticut Regiment, and forty men from Company F, One Hundred and Sixtieth New York, was ordered to steam through Grand Lake to the mouth of Bayou Teche. The object was to make a sort of reconnoissance in that vicinity. and to discover, if possible, the correctness of a report in circulation, that the rebels had a force of three hundred infantry and two pieces of artillery on the small island between Grand Lake and the Atchafalaya River. Lieutenant Pickering Dodge Allen, Aid-de-Camp to General Weitzel, accompanied the boat, and he likewise was ordered to gather all possible information regarding the strength and position of the enemy from the negroes along the banks of the stream. Captain Peterson continued to push on beyond the mouth of the Teche, in order to pass down the Atchafalaya River, which was in direct violation of General Weitzel's orders. Lieutenant Allen then asked Captain Peterson what he would do in case he was suddenly attacked by a rebel battery. He replied he was not afraid of any batteries they had and that he could blow any six of their batteries to pieces. Another object of this expedition was to discover if the rebel steamer Dart had run out of the Teche, as it was rumored by **secesh.**

Not more than an hour after the conversation alluded **to** above had taken place, when being just above Pattersonville, Captain Peterson saw a **body of** the enemy's cavalry and one or two sections of light artillery on the shore. Lieutenant Allen then advised Captain Peterson to turn back **and** avoid, if possible, a conflict with them, but Captain Peterson would not regard the protestation of Lieutenant Allen **but** kept on up the bayou, and, when **he got within range, he** opened upon the rebels with his thirty-pound pivot rifled gun. The rebels at once replied with earnestness, getting their light batteries into a raking position and sending their three hundred Texas cavalry, dismounted, to shower their **leaden** hail upon our gunners. The fire of these Texas sharp-shooters was terrific, and, as their deadly balls began to whistle over the decks, it told fearfully **upon** our men. The gunners being completely exposed to the fire **of the** rebel sharp-shooters, it was but the work of a few minutes **to** pick off every man who dared to show himself on deck.

The rebels imitated the strategy of General Weitzel, as he exhibited it in his attack on the rebel gunboat "Cotton," which he compelled the rebels to burn. The plan **was** for each section of artillery to range themselves in such a position as to command the whole surface of the Diana. Captain Peterson continued to fight them bow on, all his guns being on the bow **of the Diana,** and still retreating slowly with his boat, when the fatal bullet completed its errand of death, and Captain Peterson, who was standing in the pilot-house, rushed out and shouted, "Great God, .

they have killed me," falling a lifeless corpse on the deck. Lieutenant Pickering Dodge Allen then assumed command of the Diana, and slowly began to retreat down the Atchafalaya River towards Brashear City. The rebels seemed infuriated at this attempt to escape, and they fired with fearful rapidity, using artillery and rifles with good execution.

The grape and canister of the enemy completely cut away the bulwarks of the Diana. One shot penetrated the escape pipe, which enveloped the boat in scalding steam. The tiller rope, and bell-wires communicating with the engineers' room, were also shot away. The escape of the steam made it impossible to distinguish any object. Executive-officer Hall of the Diana, having been killed in the early part of the engagement, the command then devolved upon Lieutenant Pickering Dodge Allen, who found it impossible to get the sailors to stand by the guns, and the soldiers, seeing the vastly superior force of the enemy and the dead and dying laying around the deck, were in a measure disheartened.

The battery used by the rebels was an old Valverde battery, formerly in the regular service of the United States. In the absence of Captain Sayers, the commander of the battery, it was under the command of Lieutenant Nettles. The Texas sharp-shooters belonged to Wallar's Texas Battalion, and are the same body of desperadoes who boarded the Harriet Lane off Galveston. They are a disorganized mob, under no military discipline whatever, paying no regard to the orders of officers, but fighting and roaming at their own pleasure. They were mounted on mules, with a few creole ponies among them. It was the same body of desperadoes who were driven into the swamps by our troops sixty miles above New Orleans last August. In the above engagement they lost all their horses, many of whom they drove into the swamp in order to aid their escape, from whence it was impossible to extricate a number of them, and our men were obliged to leave them there to starve to death.

It seems that they have never received another supply of horses, owing, no doubt, to the great scarcity of good animals in the so-called Confederacy. Some of these fellows carried immense bowie knives, two and three feet long.

Mr. Dudley, the pilot of the Diana, after the tiller ropes were cut away and the wires connecting with engineers' rooms severed by shot, went to what is called the fighting wheel and endeavored to back down the Diana by her wheels, as her rudder was shot away. While he was standing on the ladder, giving verbal instructions to the engineers below as to which wheel should be used, a solid shot cut the ladder in two and knocked him overboard.

Previous to this he was fearful that the rebs might capture the Diana and he, being a Louisianian, would be hung, if captured, so he threw himself overboard. Finding himself in the water, he rose to the surface and looking up he espied the white flag, which told him that the boat's crew had surrendered and that he was in a very unhealthy place if caught. He swam to an island, a distance of nearly a mile, with three negroes who had also jumped overboard from the Diana, and after a short rest, he began his tramp of eight or nine miles to our fortifications at Brashear City. Mr. Dudley had a terrible time in escaping, being obliged to wade through swamps where the most venomous reptiles

9*

abounded in numbers. He was compelled to use a club to beat off the moccason snakes, which were remarkably numerous. Finally, with blistered and bleeding feet, Mr. Dudley and the three negroes managed to reach the edge of Grand Lake, and seizing an old dilapidated boat the party escaped to our pickets on Saturday night.

While Lieutenant Pickering Dodge Allen was below in the engineers' room, giving some orders in regard to the boat, one of the sailors hauled down the American flag. On coming up he looked for the flag, but it was down. Again raising it to the topmast, the lieutenant said: "*There, let that flag float where it is, so long as one man remains on board the Diana!*" After this there seemed to be a mutinous spirit prevailing among the sailors, who refused to obey Lieutenant Allen, as he was not a naval officer. Finding it impossible to have the guns loaded, and insubordination exhibited, he was reluctantly compelled to order the hoisting of the white flag.

Lieutenant Allen is praised by all on board, and the best evidence of his bravery is a sight of his uniform, which is completely riddled and hanging in shreds. At one time during the engagement the lieutenant was obliged to go below, and when passing through the cabin three solid shots came tearing through, scattering a perfect shower of splinters. Three round shot passed completely through the pilot house.

The moment the white flag was raised, the rebels steamed down their two gunboats, the Era No. 2—whose smoke stacks, singular to relate, are painted white—and the Hart. The Texans were not long in boarding the Diana, and they were no sooner on board than they began to rob the prisoners of all their private effects. The Texans robbed Captain Peterson and Executive-officer Hall, and all the dead, of their boots and shoes.

Captain Peterson had four or five hundred dollars in United States currency in his pocket, which the rebels took charge of for their own private use. Captain Peterson was killed in the pilot house, and was the first man shot. A ball penetrated his heart. Executive-officer Hall was shot through the chest, and lived but two hours after he was wounded. Lieutenant Dolliver was killed instantly, a discharge of canister completely disemboweling him. Captain Hewitt, senior army officer on board, Company F, One Hundred and Sixtieth New York Volunteers, was struck on the scalp with a piece of shell. The wound of itself was not dangerous, but the violent concussion has completely paralyzed him and he is not expected to recover. The Diana was plated with thin iron around her boilers, but was only protected against musketry.

The rebels have secured a valuable prize, for the Diana had a fine armament, consisting of five guns, all mounted on her bow, one thirty pounder rifled pivot, two thirty-two pounders, smooth bore, and two twelve pounders, one rifled and one smooth bore. She had on board a large supply of ammunition.

The captain of the Calhoun, which lay at Brashear City, hearing the firing, started to ascertain the cause, when the pilot ran her aground, where she remained until two o'clock on Sunday morning. Thirty tons of coal and large quantities of ammunition were thrown overboard to lighten her off.

Had the rebels known of the disaster, she also would have been lost.

Lieutenant Dolliver, who was killed, was a native of Cape Cod, Massachusetts.

BRASHEAR CITY, APRIL 16, 1863.

DEAR FATHER,—I arrived here yesterday from Franklin, which place was taken the day previous by our forces, before Captain Jewett, Lieutenant Francis and myself could be removed. I am almost well, but not at all strong. The doctors say I have recovered very rapidly and that I must have a fine constitution. I expect to be able to join the brigade in two weeks, if not sooner. The Diana was burned by the rebels; her guns will all be recovered; her men were all captured. Her captain was Semmes, a son of the commander of the Alabama. The Queen of the West was destroyed by our gunboats in Grand Lake. Her captain, Fuller (the same who commanded the Cotton), six other officers, and over one hundred men were captured; the rest, from twenty to thirty, were killed or drowned. Our land forces have taken about six hundred prisoners. I received the best of treatment while a prisoner. Have no time to write to-day, but will soon send a long letter, with an account of my late experiences.

NEW ORLEANS, APRIL 21, 1863.

DEAR FATHER AND MOTHER,—Your letter of April tenth arrived to-day. You will have heard of my having been recaptured before this, as I wrote you a few lines the day after arriving at Brashear City. The fight on the Diana was a very hard one. We were surrounded by a force of several times our own number, consisting of six companies of Texan rangers (Waller's battalion), two Arizona cavalry companies, one battery of field pieces, and two companies of the Twenty-Eighth Louisiana Infantry. Our soldiers were on the lower deck. When three of the four officers of the boat were killed, many of the sailors jumped into the hold, and this example was followed by many of the soldiers. On the upper deck were six officers all the time, and at first seven; five of these were killed or wounded; and of the thirty-two men there, fifteen were killed or wounded; on the lower deck a few were killed and several wounded. The boat was fought nearly two hours, and when surrendered was hard aground and the steam-pipe cut. I was very weak when taken, and was left at Dr. Grout's, in Pattersonville, until our forces landed on that side of Berwick Bay, when I was moved to Camp Bisland, seven miles above, and after three days was sent to Franklin, where we had excellent quarters in a new hospital. I was treated with the greatest kindness all the time; while at Camp Bisland it was difficult to get enough to eat, but the rest of the time we had every thing we could expect.

When their army retreated from Franklin we were ordered to move, on the transport Cornie, for New Iberia. On getting a few miles above Franklin it was ascertained that General Grover's forces had possession of the bayou. One of General Sibley's Staff then ordered the boat to return to Franklin. Captain Jewett, of the One Hundred and Sixtieth

New York, was the only prisoner on board beside myself, and he was unable to stand up, having been shot in the head and one side paralyzed. On arriving at Franklin, on the return, the confusion was very great, so that I left the boat. She had on her seventy or eighty confederate wounded soldiers and our guard of a corporal and three privates. I went up into the town; soon after this three or four of Perkins' cavalry passed through; I took a revolver from one of them and let them go on, they being a mile or more in advance of our cavalry. I then returned to the boat, where there were no arms, she being under the hospital flag, and found the wounded men were being removed, so demanded the surrender of the boat, which was immediately done. I was the only person on board armed, so of course had no trouble. I then took a wagon and went to meet the General, and found our brigade two or three miles in advance of the rest of the force. The confederate army was then demoralized and in full retreat.

We have taken about two thousand prisoners, and destroyed the gunboats Queen of the West, Stevens and Diana. The Stevens was a very strong boat, and was formerly called the Hart. Our gunboats destroyed the Queen of the West, and they have just taken the rebel fort at Bute la Rose, on the Atchafalaya, with a small force of two captains, four lieutenants and sixty men. Had the original plan been carried out our success would have been even more complete. I do not think there will be another fight here, of consequence, for several weeks, if so soon. I arrived in this city on Saturday. My wounds are healing rapidly, and I hope to join the General in eight or ten days. The steamer Marion, on board of which vessel my clothes and money were, has been wrecked, and it is doubtful if I ever receive them, although there seems to be a chance that they may be saved. Was the money insured? I had a small shot pass through my thumb without breaking the bone; the minnie ball came from one side (we being surrounded), striking me nearly in the middle of the back, passing under the skin a little way into my shoulder, then under the blade, then turned down my arm for about three inches, when it came out near the surface of the skin and lodged. I will send you some New Orleans papers by this mail, and a few postage stamps for M—— and L——. Will write again in a week.

POSTSCRIPT, 24TH APRIL.—I have lost the Era, with the description of General Banks' expedition in Attakapas, so send the Picayune, which is the secesh organ here, or as much so as it thinks it prudent to be. I am improving, growing stronger every day, but my arm will not be strong for a long while, and probably never will be as strong as before. I expect to join the General next week. This is the anniversary of the surrender of the city.

Through the New Orleans Era we were put in possession of important information regarding the operations of General Banks in the Teche country, which is here printed as copied at the time by the Boston Journal :—

The latest news from the front of our army on the Teche is of the same encouraging character as heretofore. On

Friday night General Banks reached Vermillionville, previous to which, however, a sanguinary and spirited fight took place at the crossing of Vermillion Bayou, a short distance this side of the village.

At this place the rebels posted a force of over one thousand infantry and strong batteries of artillery in ambush. Fire was opened upon the advance of General Banks' army from the whole force of the enemy. The fight raged furiously for some time, but resulted finally, after considerable loss on both sides, in the giving way of the rebels and the crossing of our troops.

It was reported that General Banks would undoubtedly be in Opelousas soon with his whole army.

Accounts from that part of the country state that the fortifications at Bute la Rose have been reduced by our fleet, and that the place is in our possession. At this place, as will be seen by the correspondence below, the rebels had, besides their land batteries, the ram William H. Webb.

Our correspondent details the operations as they occurred after the attack on the fortifications of Bethel Place. After the second day's fight the intrenchments were evacuated, leaving in our possession two pieces of artillery, and a large quantity of ammunition, &c.

As the army advanced, they came up with a force under General Grover which had been engaged in a desperate fight, which is described. It was in General Grover's engagement that most of the prisoners were taken.

Our forces have captured over five hundred head of horses, mules and cattle, which are of incalculable value to the captors at this juncture of affairs.

This expedition of General Banks, up the Teche country, so far has proved to be the most important and productive of satisfactory results of any that we have had to record since he has assumed the command of the Department of the Gulf. Our army is rolling like a ball of fire through the finest portion of Louisiana. When the rebels are thoroughly driven out of the Opelousas country, the backbone of the rebellion will be very much broken so far as this State is concerned.

It appears from the following letter (accompanying the foregoing), dated "In the field above New Iberia, April 17, 1863," that a two days fight occurred at the fortifications of Bethel Place previous to the events narrated. Of the operations of these days the Journal had received no account. The letter proceeds :—

At half past eleven o'clock on the night of the thirteenth instant, Colonel Kimball, of the Fifty-Third Massachusetts, heard the enemy making preparations for evacuating his intrenchments. The moving of the artillery and baggage wagons, packing and mailing of boxes, and drivers cursing their mules could be distinctly heard by the advanced pickets of Colonel Gooding's brigade. Colonel Kimball immediately notified Colonel Gooding of the fact, and he in turn sent word to Major-General Banks.

No special movement was made in pursuit of the enemy until early the next morning, when General Emory ordered a portion of his command to fire into the breastworks, to make sure that they were evacuated. But at this time

10

Colonel Kimball had entered the works on the right, and immediately planted the national colors upon the parapet.

An advance of the whole column now took place, General Weitzel's division leading the van. Upon entering the works, the scene on every hand gave the fullest evidence of bloody work the day before. Their unburied dead were lying around on all sides. Within an area of fifty feet thirty horses lay dead on the field.

There were found in the rebel works one thirty-two-pounder smooth bore cannon and a fine twelve-pounder rifled brass howitzer. This latter piece, with its caisson, was being drawn over a bridge across a ditch to the rear of the works when a solid shot, from one of our thirty-pounder Parrotts, struck the bed of the piece and threw it with the caisson into the ditch where it now lies.

Large stores of all kinds of ammunition and some Enfield rifles and a few small arms were found in the works, having been abandoned by the enemy. The remnants of a hasty meal were found scattered around near the cannon. In one place the earthworks were torn up by a bursting shell, and the earth in many places was very much ploughed up by the iron missiles of death. The wildest enthusiasm prevailed among our troops as they entered this rebel stronghold.

The army marched on the first day to a point just above Pattersonville, where it was learned that the prisoners taken from the Diana had been sent up to Franklin.

At Pattersonville, and for a short distance beyond there, the advance was annoyed by the rear guard of the retreating enemy, consisting of one hundred cavalry and three pieces of artillery. Our van was frequently fired upon, but did not retreat out of range until the second day's march, when, at one time finding themselves out of sight of the main body, the men in front fell back, or waited until the whole force came up, when the march was resumed. The town of Franklin was reached on Wednesday. Before the day was out, over two hundred prisoners were brought in and quartered in the Court House. By the next night the number had increased to over five hundred, including whole companies who were marched in at once. By a singular good fortune, three of the officers who were taken on the Diana were recaptured at this place.

When Jefferson Davis first made the proposition in the State of Louisiana that every man unwilling to fight for the Confederacy should leave the State, a Mr. Smith of Louisville had not time enough to leave with a light-draft steamer in his possession, and it was confiscated on the Ouachita. Its name was Cornie. Since that time it has been employed to transport rebel troops and army stores. For the last two months it was constantly employed in carrying salt from the mines, seven miles southwest of New Iberia, to the junction of the Teche and Cahawba bayous. From this point the salt has been transported to Alexandria, and by way of Red River to Vicksburg, Port Hudson and other places occupied by the rebels. On the twelfth instant, early in the morning, the Cornie left New Iberia with a lot of ammunition for the rebels at Camp Bisland. Upon reaching that place the boat was detained to carry away the sick and wounded in case of any emergency. On the next night she received orders to get up steam and leave at once with the wounded. Accordingly, seventy-five wounded, some fatally, and also as many sick men, were placed on board, and the boat left for the hospital at New Iberia. Only one surgeon was sent up with the wounded. Upon reaching Franklin orders were given to burn and destroy all the boats. The sick could not be removed, and so a hospital flag was raised and an attempt made to pass General Grover's command. After going a mile and a half above Franklin the Cornie met the Diana, and was ordered to return to Franklin, land the wounded, and burn the boat. On reaching that place, Lieutenant Allen, of General Weitzel's Staff, a wounded prisoner from the Diana, stepped up to the captain and demanded its surrender. "Take charge of her, sir, and hoist your flag on her," was the only and immediate reply.

Doctor Alice, of the Diana, at once secured the services of other Federal surgeons, and the sick and wounded were placed in a hospital under his charge.

By this fortunate capture, Lieutenant Allen, of Weitzel's Staff, Captain Jewett, of the One Hundred and Sixtieth New York Regiment, and Lieutenant Alice, of the Diana, were retaken, and immediately commenced performing every service for the unfortunate sufferers.

On the day the Cornie was captured the rebels burned the Newsboy, a large stern-wheeler, the Gossamer, stern-wheel, larger than the Newsboy, and the Era, Number Two, the largest of all; the gunboat Diana was burned at the same time; all of them at Franklin.

The next day, at New Iberia, the Louisa, the Derby, the Uncle Tommy (side-wheel, formerly a ferry-boat at Plaque-mine), the Blue Hammock (side-wheel), and the gunboat Hart were all burned. The Cricket was sunk at the junction of the Teche and Cahawba bayous. The gunboat Hart was one of the best and fastest gunboats in the rebel navy. She carried one thirty two pound rifled cannon forward, and another like it aft, and two small smooth-bore twenty-four pound brass pieces under her casement. Her machinery and bulkheads were protected by three-inch railroad iron, the heaviest kind in use. She had two splendid engines aboard, of twenty-inch cylinder, seven feet stroke. There were four double-flue boilers on the boat. She was commenced upon the day after the Lurning of the Cotton, but for some reason had not been finished until recently. She now lies with her ruined hulk across the Teche, above New Iberia.

Large stores of provisions and ammunition were destroyed with these boats, including some twenty thousand pounds of bacon and nearly a thousand cases of ammunition.

We are in possession of certain information with reference to the long cherished designs of the enemy. They had purposed sending the gunboat Hart down the Teche, together with the Picayune, her transport. On the Cahawba they were about sending the Marietta and the B. L. Hodge. From the Red River, the Queen of the West, the Webb, the W. Roberts, the Grand Duke and the Roebuck were to come. Two rams, building at Shreveport, they were to send, if finished,—one of them, half solid, built purposely for butting, was to come round by way of the Mississippi and attack the boats at New Orleans. Those on the Teche were to come directly down that bayou to Brashear City. Those on the Cahawba and the Red River were to come down the Atchafalaya to the same point, and, after its capture, to go around by the Balize and another route to New Orleans. They were to rally their infantry at the same time at Plaquemine, and take the railroad running from Brashear City. On the thirteenth it was the enemy's design to retreat as far as Alexandria, about one hundred miles west of Opelousas, and make a stand. Kirby Smith was to meet them there with reinforcements and assume command of them.

As the main body of our troops reached Franklin, the news of General Grover's recent operations was brought to General Banks. General Grover's division was in camp at Brashear City when the remainder of the forces started from Berwick City.

The division had been ordered to remain, for the purpose of constituting an expedition to attack the enemy in the rear at the same time the main body drove him from the earthworks below.

Early on Sunday morning, the twelfth instant, the whole division embarked on board the gunboats Calhoun, Clifton, Estrella and Arizona, and the transports St. Mary, Laurel Hill, Quinebaug, Southern Merchant and Segur.

Proceeding up the bay, through Grand Lake Pass and Grand Lake, by a cross bayou, they reached Irish Bend, on the Teche, a bend like that of an ox yoke about three miles west of Franklin.

The First Louisiana Regiment was the first to land. It had hardly stepped ashore when an attack was made upon it by the rebels with two pieces of artillery and two hundred infantry. Some were killed on both sides during the firing which immediately followed. The enemy were compelled to

fall back. Upon reaching the Teche several rifle shots were
fired by the rebels. They attempted to prevent the approach
of our troops. This attempt likewise failed before the sharp
firing of our men, and the rebels were driven still further
back. Our men crossed the Teche and bivouacked for the
night. The next morning, at an early hour, they started
toward Franklin. While marching along the levee road,
upon reaching a point two miles from Franklin, on what is
called Irish Bend, they again met the enemy. There was a
cross road meeting the main, and in this the rebel artillery
was planted, commanding all the country about there.

As the troops came up, to their right was a thick forest
of large trees, behind which the enemy was concealed, having also a wooden fence between them and their opposers.
Preparations were made at once for a desperate attack.
One of their number, now a prisoner, remarked: "We know
that we have got to fight hard or be taken prisoners."

The Twenty-Fifth Connecticut Regiment was the first to
engage the enemy. It occupied the centre of the line of
battle, having the Twenty-Sixth Maine Regiment on the
right and the Thirteenth Connecticut Regiment on the left,
and supported by the Twelfth Maine Regiment.

It was deployed as skirmishers on the left of the road,
and thus marched until abreast of the woods, and then,
while under a sharp fire from the enemy, the line gradually
swung round until it faced the woods, letting the enemy get
to their rear. This accomplished, an attempt was made to
capture our artillery, without success, although the regiment gradually fell back until it received support from the
Ninety-First New York.

The Twenty-Fifth Connecticut Regiment was ordered into action on the left of the line, and in the advance. They met the enemy awaiting their approach in a piece of woods, where their artillery was supported by a strong force of infantry and cavalry. When a charge was ordered, to force the rebels from their position and to take their artillery, the Thirteenth had to charge through a ploughed field and over two fences. Notwithstanding these obstacles this regiment succeeded in capturing two caissons, six horses, two swords and a splendid flag from the enemy. The flag was of fine silk, six feet in length, bordered with rich silver tinsel, and bore upon it the inscription, " The Ladies of Franklin to the St. Mary's Cannoneers."

Soon after the charge of the Thirteenth the enemy fell back defeated. The force opposed to us was not large, but had the advantage of position and of making a surprise. The total force of the rebels, both here and at the batteries below, did not exceed ten thousand men. Our loss was considerable, and that of the enemy must have corresponded with ours. Sibley's brigade was included in this number,— two regiments of Texas cavalry, Captain Sims' battery and the Valverde and Pelican batteries. The whole force was under the command of General Dick Taylor, son of the late Zachary Taylor. At this moment the whole force is retreating from our troops, demoralized and hopeless of their cause.

By the time our troops had arrived at New Iberia, nearly five hundred and sixty horses, mules and beef cattle had been collected, and were placed in kraals along the wayside. Their numbers were so rapidly augmented, by the constant seizures from the plantations bordering the road, that it became necessary to establish additional places for their safe keeping. The mules were found very useful to the regimental surgeons in the transportation of the sick. Some fine blooded horses were made to replace the more jaded animals bestrode by officers.

Seven miles west of New Iberia, and near Vermilion Bay, in the middle of a mud lake, thick grown with flag and cane, rises a ledge of solid rock, the surface and depth of which have not been discovered. From this mine thousands of dollars worth of the best of salt has been daily sent away for the use of the rebel army. Negroes were employed to blast and break it up, some being ground at the mine. It is reported that the rebels paid four and a half cents per pound for what they took away. When our troops reached Iberia, a regiment was sent up to take possession and destroy the tools and machinery there.

When our gallant men are facing death upon the field, risking their lives at every moment, it is gratifying to know that skilful hands are ready to bind up their wounds and render every service to comfort the bed of pain. During the engagements of Sunday and Monday, Dr. D. L. Rogers, acting medical director of the department, labored hard to provide every possible convenience for the wounded, establishing hospitals, and keeping an ambulance corps in constant readiness to convey the wounded from the field.

For the time two hospitals were established, one at Brashear City and one at New Iberia, whence the wounded will be conveyed to New Orleans at the first opportunity.

A hospital was established at Franklin, after the return of the Cornie, and filled with the rebel sick and wounded. Dr. Rogers left it in charge of Dr. Alice, formerly surgeon of the Diana. Afterward, the very wise plan was adopted of paroling the wounded and giving them into the hands of their friends.

Connected with the advance of the expedition, nothing more plainly indicated the demoralized condition of the rebel army than the rapid capture of their disheartened soldiers. During the actions of Bethel Place and Irish Bend, along the route taken by the defeated, and at Franklin, New Iberia and other places crowds of them have fallen into our hands. Already nearly fifteen hundred prisoners have been taken, including some characters well known in New Orleans.

A short distance below New Iberia our forces discovered a foundry by the wayside, an examination of which disclosed the fact that it had been used for casting shot and shell. It had, however, been abandoned, with all its machinery, tools and a quantity of shot and shell.

From letters found in Captain Fuller's possession it is known that the Webb, on the thirteenth, was at Bute la Rose. The Marietta was on the Red River, as also the transport Grand Duke. It appears that the rebels were not informed of the proposed attack on Bethel Place. This letter of General Taylor to Captain Fuller was written on the twelfth of April, at the very moment our forces were before the enemy's works. It very properly recommends to Captain Fuller that he postpone the attack upon Brashear City. So it has come to light that we had delayed so long in attacking the enemy, that he was bold enough to organize an expedition against us.

Concerning these operations, the New Orleans Picayune referred to by Pickering said:—

The severest blow to the confederates was the destruction of the ram Queen of the West by the United States naval force in Grand Lake, consisting of the steamers Arizona, Estrella and Calhoun, the whole under command of Lieutenant Commander A. P. Cooke, United States Navy. It was the intention of the commander of the Queen of the West to destroy, if possible, the Federal fleet by ramming them, and in this manner prevent the army of General Banks recrossing the Atchafalaya to Brashear City, and cutting off their supplies; but he was destined to be mistaken in his calculations, for a shell from one of the Federal gunboats burst among a quantity of loose powder on board of the Queen of the West, which caused a terrific explosion, whereby her machinery was disabled and the boat set on fire. She was abandoned by her officers and crew, and burnt until the flames reached her magazine, which blew up, scattering the fragments of this famous vessel in every direction. The Queen of the West was commanded by Captain Fuller, well known as the late commander of the Confederate gunboat Cotton. He was injured by the explosion, and is now a prisoner in this city. The total complement of officers and men on board the Queen of the West, at the time of her going into action, was about one hundred and fifty; of these about ninety have been taken prisoners, the balance are undoubtedly killed or drowned. There is no doubt that the destruction of this vessel exercised an important influence upon the subsequent movements of the Confederate army. She was the right arm of their defence, and her destruction undoubtedly caused a retreat of the forces of General Taylor much sooner than they would had she succeeded in maintaining herself uninjured.

The United States gunboat Clifton, Lieutenant Crocker commanding, mounting eight very heavy guns, played a very important part on Bayou Teche, in throwing heavy nine-inch and thirty-two-pound shells into the Confederate ranks,—she having removed the obstructions placed in the bayou, or succeeding in passing around them, compelled the destruction of the gunboat Diana (recently captured from the Federal forces near Pattersonville). Captain Semmes, commanding a Confederate field battery, a gentleman well known in this community, was on board the Diana when her destruction became a matter of necessity. He was captured, and is now a prisoner in this city. The Confederate gunboat Hart, or Stevens, as she has lately been named, was destroyed, together with several steam transports, to prevent their falling into the hands of the United States forces.

LAKE CHICOT, LA., MAY 1, 1863.

DEAR FATHER AND MOTHER,—

You will probably be surprised to hear from me on this lake. I am in command of this boat for a few days, and have a section of artillery (two brass howitzers) and one hundred sharp-shooters from the Fourth Massachusetts. We are to accompany Captain Cooke's gunboat fleet to the mouth of the Red River, to communicate with Admiral Farragut. This boat is the Cornie, the one that surrendered to me at Franklin, and is well protected with cotton. We do not expect much opposition, if any; the only point where there is likely to be any is at Semmesport, near the mouth of Red River. At last dates they had a light battery and two or three hundred infantry there; they have probably left before this. They would not be able to make much of a stand against the gunboats we have, should they make the attempt. This boat is sent to bring back the despatches and take them to General Banks. We hope to hear from General Grant, above Red River.

Doctor Benedict would not allow me to join the brigade for a few days, so I obtained command of this boat from General Banks. I have a good room, and if the expedition is, as I think it will be, successful, shall enjoy the trip. My health was never better, but I am not yet as strong as usual. My money, by the Marion, has arrived; the box is lost. The two hundred you sent to Lieutenant Bowles, for my use when a prisoner, came also; this I have, as the money sent me came from the Quarter-Master's Department—was Confederate currency—and as I used but a very small part, it was returned on my release. I have had to purchase clothing, as I lost one entire suit, it being completely torn to pieces by splinters, on the Diana, and I had to cut up all my shirts to get them on, while wounded. About half the remainder of my underclothing was lost when I was moved in such haste from Pattersonville, on the advance of our

11

troops. I will get new ones in the city, as it will take too long to replace them from home.

I shall leave this at Bute la Rose, where we have a regiment. Was I not very fortunate in getting away from the secesh? I received better treatment than their prisoners ordinarily received from us, and suffered but little after the first day or two. I hope we shall be fortunate enough to catch some of their transports on our way up the Atchafalaya. We are now going into the mouth of the river, so I wish to be on deck. I hope to get back to Brashear in a week or ten days, but may possibly be longer away and will write as soon as we return.

My letters were very uninteresting, and I suppose the reason was that you thought they would have to be sent me by flag of truce and read by the enemy, as of course they would have been if I had remained a prisoner in their hands. General Weitzel is more popular than ever; I am very fortunate in being on his Staff. We left Brashear this morning and now are fifty miles above there, a quarter of the distance to the Red River. Good bye.

Yours, affectionately.

BRASHEAR CITY, MAY 8, 1863.

DEAR FATHER AND MOTHER,—

You should have received a letter from me, written on Chicot Lake about a week since. I returned here in three or four days, going first to Opelousas and seeing the General. On our way up, when about forty miles from the mouth of Red River, we met the Arizona returning, the having already been to the Admiral. Captain Dunham, of General Banks' Staff, came on board the Cornie, and we started immediately for the General. There is small chance of fighting at Alexandria; it will probably surrender on the appearance of our forces.

Lieutenant Bowles showed me your letter to him. You appear much troubled about me; but the tidings of my escape will have reached you long before this. My wounds are healed, and I expect to leave here for the General the day after to-morrow. Was not Howard Dwight's murder a horrible affair? His younger brother, Charles, goes home with the body.* You will have heard of Colonel Grierson's splendid cavalry raid through Missis-

---

* "Captain Howard Dwight, Assistant Adjutant-General to Brigadier-General George L. Andrews, was murdered to-day, under the following circumstances: He had passed a point at which there is a turn in the Bayou Boeuf, when he was ordered to halt, and where his previous experience authorized him to suppose that he was in little or no danger. The account given by an eyewitness shows that so far was he from suspecting danger, that on being ordered to halt, instead of putting spurs to his horse, which would probably have insured his escape, he deliberately turned, and walked his horse back to see what it meant. On reaching the end of the bayou he found himself confronted by three rebel cavalrymen, who were on the opposite side of the bayou, at the water's edge; immediately their three rifles were brought to bear upon him. In this position he submitted to the necessity of the case, and surrendered himself a prisoner. One of the rebels then said 'He's a damned Yankee; let 's kill him.' Captain Dwight calmly replied, 'You must not fire; I am your prisoner.' Again the rebels said to each other, 'Kill the damned Yankee,' and immediately one of them fired. The ball passed through Captain Dwight's brain, killing him instantly. The scene was witnessed by two boys, who remained by the body until the arrival of our cavalry, who were but three minutes behind when the event occurred, and, hearing the report of the rifle, hastened forward."—(*Official Account.*)

sippi. My mail by the last steamer was sent to the front, so I shall not get it for several days. I expect to see W—— next week. It is nearly five months since I have seen him. We are having very fine weather. Yesterday and to-day the temperature has been as low as at home, very unusually cool for this country in May. More than six hundred of the prisoners captured on the Teche have taken the oath to our government. About twelve thousand bales of cotton were captured in the Teche country. The papers have absurd stories of its being two hundred thousand bales. Near this quantity is said to be on the Red River; part of this will unquestionably be burned. All things look favorably in this department. For all military movements I must refer you to the newspapers.

I received a hundred dollars by Adams's Express day before yesterday. Do not send the usual supply of money this month, as I have enough, but send again in June. If you have already done so, before receipt of this, omit the June remittance. Good bye.

Yours, affectionately.

BRASHEAR CITY, MAY 26, 1863.

DEAR FATHER,—

It is a long time since I have heard from you. Our brigade mails appear to have been lost, as no one has had a letter for four or five mails. I left this place two or three weeks since, and went to Alexandria, where I joined the General, but I was taken with the malarial fever, so common in this country, the day after leaving here, probably partly owing to my not having been very strong. I went from Alexandria to Semmesport and Bayou Sarah, just north of Port Hudson, but was compelled to return from there, as I was very weak. The doctors have advised my going north for a few weeks. I have sent in an application for a short furlough; it is strongly endorsed by General Weitzel and our medical director, Dr. Benedict. The General is to take it himself to General Banks, so there is scarcely a doubt of my getting it. I ought to receive it in a few days; certainly in a week. As I expect to see you soon I will not write more, but will in a few days. I am better; am not much sick, but quite weak, and expect to be well before getting North. Good bye.

Yours, affectionately. P. D. A.

HEAD-QUARTERS SECOND BRIGADE, FIRST DIVISION, NINETEENTH CORPS,
Semmesport, La., May 23, 1863.

LIEUTENANT-COLONEL RICHARD B. IRWIN,
Assistant Adjutant-General,—

SIR,—I respectfully ask leave of absence from this Department for sixty days, to enable me to visit the North to recover my health.

I have the honor to enclose surgeon's certificate, showing my present inability to discharge my duties, and the need I have of a change of climate.

I am, sir, very respectfully,

Your obedient servant,

PICKERING D. ALLEN,
Lieutenant and Aid-de-Camp.

11*

HEAD-QUARTERS SECOND BRIGADE, FIRST DIVISION,
In the Field, May 23, 1863.

Lieutenant P. D. Allen having applied to me for a certificate, upon which to ground an application for leave of absence, I certify that I have carefully examined this officer and find that he was wounded and taken prisoner on board the Diana at Pattersonville, La., March 28, 1863, that he has not fully recovered from the effects of his wound, and that he is now suffering from fever and debility resulting from the wound and subsequent exposure; and in consequence thereof he is unfit for duty. I further certify that in my opinion he will not be fit for duty in a less time than sixty days from this date, and that a sea voyage will conduce to his recovery.   M. D. BENEDICT,

Surgeon Seventy-Fifth New York Volunteers, and
Medical Director General Weitzel's Brigade.

The facts in this case are so well known that I think I only need say that justice demands that this deserving officer be granted the favor he asks.

G. WEITZEL,

Brigadier-General United States Volunteers.

Before Port Hudson, May 26, 1863.

Leave granted for twenty days, with permission to apply for an extension of forty.

By command of MAJOR-GENERAL BANKS,

RICHARD B. IRWIN,

Assistant Adjutant-General.

When Pickering's letter came, we did not from its contents suppose that he was much ill; nor was he at that time. He was only weak, and we anticipated that the sea air would restore him to his usual vigor. We were expecting to hear of his arrival at New York, when, on the morning of June thirteenth, a letter from a friend who went out in the steamer to New Orleans as fellow passenger with him was received. The following is part of its contents :—

Pickering partially recovered from his wound, and would insist on going to the front in the performance of his duty, before he was really strong enough, and the consequence was an attack of fever, which turned to typhoid, and terminated his young life, on Tuesday evening, June second, at Brashear City. I was not with him, nor did I know of his danger. He was surrounded by kind friends, and was at the house of Captain Fitch, who, with his wife and Lieutenant-Commander Cooke and Mrs. Cooke and others were devoted to him, night and day. Captain Fitch brought his remains to this city, and delivered them in my charge, and you may rest assured that I have done all that his friends could have done if present, and now send them home to those who loved him best on earth, in the care of Lieutenant John G. Snow of Maine, who also has with him the remains of Captain J. B. Hubbard, of the same staff, who fell a few days before your son left us. They were true and devoted friends in life. I cannot refrain from saying, as a tribute to the memory of my young friend, that few have been here who have made more sincere friends, or that have been more beloved or respected as a brave, noble and high toned gentleman. The body is preserved in spirit, and looks so natural that I think but little change will be found to exist when it arrives. May God comfort you in your great loss.

In due time, letters were received from several other friends, which supply additional particulars relative to the closing days of Pickering's life :—

BRASHEAR CITY, LA., JUNE 3, 1863.

JOHN F. ALLEN, ESQ.,—

DEAR SIR,—There are times in the life of all men when the heart is too full of grief to unburden itself, and when the pen refuses its mission. But the task, however painful, must be performed.

Your noble son, Pickering D. Allen, whom we all so devotedly loved, has gone to his rest. Softly and sweetly he passed away, on the evening of June second, at half past six, his bedside surrounded by devoted, weeping friends. Nothing was left undone that fond hearts could do, and the gentle hands of women who love their country and its defenders smoothed his pillow and administered to his wants.

We feel his loss here too deeply for utterance. He wound himself about our hearts because he was brave, noble generous, true.

His remains were sent to New Orleans this morning, where they will be carefully embalmed and forwarded to you at the earliest possible moment.

May God in His infinite goodness give to you, and the loved ones who surround your "home hearth," strength from on high to bear this chastisement. Remember as you mourn, that yours is but one offering of the tens of thousands to the great cause of human liberty,—yours but one wounded heart.

With sorrow and sadness, I remain

Respectfully your obedient servant,

EDWARD B. LANSING,

First Lieutenant and Adjutant Seventy-Fifth New York State Volunteers.

BRASHEAR CITY, JUNE 10, 1863.

MRS. J. F. ALLEN,—

DEAR MADAM,—In this hour of deep bereavement, when your affliction seems greater than you can bear, I know full well that words of sympathy from those you have never known will fail to give you comfort. And yet, as everything pertaining to the loved and lost is dear, I thought you would be glad to hear some particulars of your noble son's last illness from those who were intimately associated with him during the last three weeks of his life. To you who knew him so well, I need not say that he wound himself very closely around our hearts during our brief, but intimate acquaintance. His high sense of honor, his gentlemanly bearing and kind heart, could not fail to win for him respect and esteem. It was not my privilege to form his acquaintance until he returned from Pattersonville.

Since that time he has formed one of our mess-family at the house of Captain Fitch, the provost marshal of this place, and seemed like an old friend. I have delayed writing this letter, hoping Mrs. Cooke, who knew him so much better than any one here, would have recovered sufficiently from her illness to write. Lieutenant-Commander Cooke was one of your son's dearest friends, and his wife was untiring in her devotion to your son; she scarcely left his bedside during his last illness, although herself quite unwell. Mr. Allen often said that but for her gentle and unremitting attentions he should be blue and homesick.

When Mr. Allen returned from Pattersonville he was very feeble, but after a few days gained rapidly during the three weeks he remained here. His anxiety to be with the General, and assist him, led him to go to the front before he had sufficiently recovered his strength. He took cold on the boat, going from Brashear to Alexandria, and as the army were without tents the General sent him on board Commodore Cooke's gunboat, and the Commodore gave him his state-room and procured good medical advice; he had some fever, but was able to keep around. At the expiration of two weeks he returned with us to Brashear, and at that time, although he had some fever every day, he was able to walk about the house and sit with us at table. He was only confined to his bed six days; he sank very rapidly from that time, and breathed out his life as quietly and peacefully as if sinking to sleep,—no sigh, no groan. Dr. Wilson, the medical director, resides with us, and saw him almost hourly; he had also the counsel of several other skilful physicians. None of them thought him dangerously ill until three days before his death. During that time he was delirious and did not realize **his situation.** His disease was not violent, but he was so prostrated from his wound that he had not sufficient vitality to combat even a slight fever. . . . I am, very truly,

MRS. J. B. VAN PETTEN.

NEW ORLEANS, JUNE 19, 1863.

MRS. ALLEN,—

MY DEAR MADAM,—Although you have heard through others of the death of your noble son, I feel that I too must write you, not only to give you more fully the *particulars* of his sickness and death, but to fulfil a promise I made him **the** day before he died; **it was** during a few moments of quiet, after having tossed about with pain and delirium, that he said to me, "Will *you* some day write my mother?" Knowing him **to be too weak** and exhausted to talk, and that he required **rest,** without questioning him **what, I** promised to do so. He expressed no other **wish,** and left no messages for you, though he often, *very* often, *spoke* of you, and was **anxious** to join you all at home.

Mrs. Allen, I am a stranger **to** you, yet I knew your *son* quite intimately, and was with him constantly the last two weeks of his life. I nursed and cared for him as tenderly as **I** could have done had he been my brother, or my *own* darling boy. It **was** a pleasure to me **to** bathe his fevered brow, cool his **parched lips, or in any** way add to his comfort; and **deprived, as he was, of your** kind care, it was a consolation to him that we could be with him to soothe and ease his pain. He suffered nothing from want of care, *every-thing* was done for him that could have been done, every wish was gratified, and every luxury a sick one could enjoy, was procured for him. We all loved him, and would have done *anything* for him. As I watched beside him, I *prayed* God to spare him to *you*, to us, but that could not be, and with all our watching, all our care and love for him, we could not stay the hand of death; his *work* was finished, and God took him home.

For the last five months I saw him almost daily, except during the time he was a prisoner; being an intimate friend of my husband, and often with him aboard ship, I met him there frequently, and situated as we were away from our homes, in an enemy's country, during such trying times there was a tie that drew us together and made our little circle seem one family, and as *such* we regarded each other. Many were the pleasant gatherings we had at the different officers' tents and many were the delightful rides we took, and our little parties were always *happy* ones. Lieutenant Allen's noble traits of character and kind pleasant manner won for him the respect and esteem of all who knew him, and now that he is gone we feel his loss deeply, and mourn for and *miss* him much. He spent some time with us after his return from Pattersonville, and before having entirely recovered the use of his arm. Being anxious to take a part in the active campaign, he applied for and was given the command of the "Cornie," the little boat *he* captured. He was to join my husband's fleet and communicate with Admiral Farragut. Before he reached the gunboats the communication had been established, and as there was nothing more *he* cared to do, he returned to us at Brashear, where he spent another week, and left us the eleventh of May to join the General, who was then **at** Alexandria. Tuesday he met him, and as they were on the march, and he not feeling well, the General advised him to remain with my husband until he should have recovered. His sickness continued, though it seemed nothing serious or alarming. The first few days he suffered from headache, with slight fever; **was** weak, and could sit **up but a** short time. The severe loss of blood from his wound prostrated him more than *he*, or any one realized. **He was with** my husband a week, and had medical attendance, and was as comfortable as could be under the circumstances. At the expiration of that time he went on board one of the transports to return again to Brashear, **where** he hoped to regain his health sufficiently to enable him to return home. It fortunately happened that we ladies were on **the boat.** We went out on a little excursion, expecting to be gone only two days; the boat was taken **to** transport troops, and we were detained a week. As soon as we saw your son we advised him to return with us, but he was *so* anxious to be with the General in **the attack on** Port Hudson, he insisted upon joining him, in an ambulance, and it was **not** until the doctor *recommended* it, that he consented to **go**; and it was *then* he applied for leave of absence.

On the boat he **had a** comfortable state-room, which he *kept* most of the time, though he took his meals with us at table. **Wednesday he** had high fever, with severe pain in his head. I bathed it **for him,** and he slept some, and rested quietly **during the night.** Thursday he was *better,*

12

and sat with us in the cabin an hour or more. Friday he was about the same, and in the evening sat with us, and watched the bombarding of Port Hudson. The excitement and exertion was too much for him, and he did not rest as well that night. Saturday we returned from Bayou Sara to Semmesport, and were obliged to leave the boat and go ashore; there we met the General, and he took us to head-quarters, and made us as comfortable as possible for the night, and Mr. Allen rested *well.* Sunday we started for Brashear; he was comfortable during the day, and rested much of the time, he seemed to *require* so much sleep. We arrived home about midnight and returned to the house, but he remained on the boat until morning, when he joined us; he appeared no worse, and we hoped he would soon be entirely recovered. His fever used to come on about nine in the morning, and seldom left him before five in the after-noon. During that time he sat up but little, and suffered with pain in his head more or less; but bathing with ice water or cologne relieved him, and he would quietly sleep. Tuesday he was about the same, and wrote a short letter home in the afternoon, and it quite fatigued him. Wednes-day he was not as well, and, for the first time, laid down on the bed, and kept his room nearly the whole day. He had no more fever, but greater pain, and his strength seemed failing. I sat beside him during the day, and fanned him while he slept, but his rest was not quiet, and did not seem to refresh him. In the evening, after Joe (his servant) had carefully bathed and rubbed him, he felt better, and slept well during the night. Thursday, he was too sick and weak to be dressed, and kept his bed all day. I was with him

much of the time, and he slept quietly, and his fever was not
as high, but at *night* he did not rest well. Friday, he was
no worse, but he had lost all relish for any food we could
prepare for him, and he took but little nourishment. **During**
the day he rested, and in the evening sent for one of the
Colonels to come see him. **All** through his sickness his
mind was with the army, and he was so interested in every
movement. There was one point, near Brashear, that *he*
did not think properly guarded, and he wished to communicate it to the Colonel. He talked with him but a short
time, yet it excited him so much he **did not rest as well**
that night. Saturday, we **saw** no change in him, **and he**
appeared no worse, but in the afternoon became delirious,
and continued so during the night, **and was** restless and
could not sleep. Sunday morning, when I went in his
room, he said to me, being conscious, "I have had such a
terrible night,"—he begged me to sit down beside him **and**
soothe him to sleep. **I** did so, and in a few moments he
was sleeping as sweetly **and** quietly as possible. I remained
with him all day, and he rested much of the **time, but was**
delirious. At night he slept well. Monday, his *delirium*
continued, yet his symptoms **were more** favorable, **but**
during the night he grew **worse,** and Tuesday morning
there was a great change in him; it shocked and pained
me to see him *so sick,* but I had *no* thought of *death.* All
the morning he was unconscious, seemed stupid, and did not
speak with us at all. **At** noon he appeared to be failing,
and it was *then,* for **the first time, I** felt he could not live.
It was a *sad,* SAD thought **to me, and** it seemed it *must* not
be. **From that time he failed as rapidly** as possible. I did

not for a moment leave him, but sat beside him, with his hand in mine, until the last throbbing of the pulse told me *all was over.* He died so quietly, so peacefully, it seemed to me he *must* be sleeping. He did *not,* nor did *we,* realize that he was so ill. He never complained or murmured, but was hopeful and patient, gentle and kind, and during his sickness never *once* forgot his "Thank you" for any attention paid him. . . .   Yours, respectfully,

FANNIE R. COOKE.

DONALDSONVILLE, LA., JULY 14, 1863.

J. F. ALLEN, ESQ., SALEM, MASS.,—

MY DEAR SIR,—I little dreamt that I would be compelled, in my second written interview with you, to treat on such a sad and painful subject as is now before you. It was my duty to announce to you his death; I could not do it. Pickering was sick when I left him at Semmesport. He was so sick that I insisted upon it that he should apply for a furlough. I procured it for him immediately after arriving at head-quarters near Port Hudson, but it did not reach him at Brashear City until within two days of his death. I, engaged in the stirring events around Port Hudson, fancied Pickering on his way home, and pictured to myself the great pleasures he would enjoy after regaining his health, and felicitated him mentally upon them, because I knew he deserved a respite.

A few mornings after his death, I received the news, whilst at my breakfast in the woods. I could not believe it at first, and even now cannot realize it, for he was as a brother. He and I were of the same age. I could not be associated with him long, and every day see his excellent virtues developed, without falling in love with them. So perfectly innocent and childlike in his manner, so brave, energetic, high toned and intelligent. He was the pet and pride of the brigade. Often he has sat on my bed, after I had retired, asked me for information and instruction in military affairs, begging me to let him perform some hazardous deed, and both of us confiding to each other our secrets, our history and experiences. I never went anywhere on any duty, or for pastime and pleasure, that Pickering was not by my side.

He was admired by all the people, whether secessionists or not, wherever we went. It was so fitting, since fate had ordained their death, that his body and that of John B. Hubbard, our mutual brother, went North together on the same vessel. In these two young men the country has suffered a great loss; I have suffered an irreparable one. If my life is spared I will verbally say more to you and yours. For the present, let us all console ourselves with the knowledge that although he is gone in body, his virtues will forever live among us.

Your associate in grief, G. WEITZEL,
Brigadier-General United States Volunteers.

NEW ORLEANS, LA., NOVEMBER 26, 1863.

MY DEAR MADAM,—

. . . I became acquainted with your son in September, 1862, as soon as General Weitzel received his brigade, and

12*

on the Lafourche campaign it chanced that we spent nearly one whole night together in the saddle. He was generally sent by General Weitzel on reconnoissances, and my regiment being a favorite one with the General and Staff, Allen and I often found ourselves on duty together. He was always cool and brave on dangerous duty, and was a very attractive companion. During the manœuvring which preceded General Banks' summer campaign, he was almost constantly in presence of the enemy in the Teche country, engaged on scouting and reconnoitring duty, and many were the plans he and I laid together for surprising or attacking the enemy's outposts. Other plans and older heads prevented our attempting some of them, but some were successful. During the month of February, especially, we were daily sailing up the lakes and bayous from Berwick's Bay, or galloping about the island on which Brashear City stands, with the ladies of our little circle.

On Sunday, February twenty-second, we went up the Atchafalaya, over the spot where he afterwards was wounded and captured. It was then considered very hazardous, but we understood our orders to require us to go through. The next attempt to pass this place was not required by the orders of General Weitzel, was made against Allen's earnest remonstrance, and resulted in the sad disaster of the capture of the Diana, and the shortening of the life of our friend. I next saw him at Franklin, where he had just raised the good old flag on the steamer Cornie, and my men gave him three warm cheers as he rode along the line. May third we went down from Opelousas to Brashear together, and met quite often until the twenty-fourth May, when I bade him

good-by for the last time as he started for *home*, and I for
the assault of Port Hudson. His application for leave of
absence was in my handwriting, but was a matter of common interest to us all, and we hoped in a few days to **hear**
of him well out of the worry of war, and on his way to the
bracing air of the North. You know the rest from those
who have told it to me, and who do not weary of talking of
our friend.   Respectfully, your friend,

W. BABCOCK,

Lieutenant-Colonel United States Volunteers.

NEW ORLEANS, DECEMBER 2, 1863.

MY DEAR MRS. ALLEN,—

. . . I have often wished to write you and tell you **how**
much I admired and respected your son, and with what deep
grief I watched the closing of his dear life. I have seldom
known one who, on an intimate and continued **acquaintance,**
disclosed such fine and rare qualities of character.

On his return to us, after having been a prisoner, he struck
us all as being greatly changed. We thought it—and it
probably was—attributable to the terrible trial **he passed**
through on the Diana. He appeared to us unusually serious,
thoughtful and earnest from that time till his death.

Often in talking, though he had no thought of the near
approach of death to himself, he said, " I am almost a fatal-
ist; I believe **when a man's** time comes **to** die, he will die,
whether it be on the battle field or **elsewhere."**

To us it was an inscrutable Providence that saved his
life on the Diana, at last, to take it, later, after suffering

wounds and sickness. This change in him, as I think of him now, seemed like a maturing for Eternity.

But he considered poor Hubbard and Wrosnowski fortunate in having so quick and painless a death. He loved Captain Hubbard very deeply, and his death fell heavily upon him. It never once occurred to us or to him that he would so quickly, and in a less fortunate way, follow his dear friend. I thought God would spare him ; he was so useful, so true, so brave, it did not seem his work could be done.

But he sank rapidly and unconsciously into his long rest; gentle, kind, grateful, affectionate, to the last. We loved him; we love his memory! God alone knows the loss to us of our friends who have fallen in this war.

Mrs. Van Petten sends her regards to you, and hopes some day to meet you. My regards to your husband and your daughters. *I* know what the loss of *such* a brother is and will be to them. Yours, very sincerely,

H. E. M. BABCOCK.

The paragraphs which follow appeared in the journals of the day :—

I regret to announce the death of Lieutenant Allen, of General Weitzel's Staff. He died at Brashear City, a few days since, of typhoid fever, after a few days illness only. His body has been brought to this city, and will be sent North in a day or two on board the steamer Fulton. The body of Captain Hubbard will also go North by the same conveyance. Lieutenant Allen was from Salem, Massachusetts, and has been in this department for a long time. He was wounded and taken prisoner when the steamer Diana was captured on Bayou Teche, and retaken when Franklin was occupied by our forces. At that time he alone compelled the surrender of the steamer Cornie with over eighty rebels on board. Lieutenant Allen was well known and highly esteemed, and his loss will be deeply regretted by all who were acquainted with him. To General Weitzel his loss will be a great blow, for he was one of the most efficient officers on his staff. He has lost three of his staff officers within the last ten days, and has, I understand, but one left.

[New York Herald's Correspondent, New Orleans, June 5.

FUNERAL OF CAPTAIN HUBBARD AND LIEUTENANT ALLEN.—Funeral services over the remains of Captain J. B. Hubbard, Assistant Adjutant-General, and Lieutenant P. D. Allen, Aid-de-Camp, of General Weitzel's Staff, will be held at No. 220 Camp Street, on Sunday morning, at ten o'clock, by Rev. Mr. Chubbuck, Post Chaplain.

Lieutenant Allen will be recollected in connection with the capture of the steamer Diana by the rebels. He afterwards, by his presence of mind, secured to the Union Army the capture of the steamer Cornie, during a time when the officers of that boat were under the influence of a panic. He fell a victim to disease brought on by unwearied attention to official duties.

Officers of the Army and Navy are respectfully invited to attend and to join in the escort; as also are the friends of the deceased in civil life.

[New Orleans Era, June 6, 1863.

[From the Essex Register, Salem, June 15—Editorial]

DEATH OF LIEUTENANT ALLEN.—The sad news was received on Saturday of the death in Louisiana of Lieutenant Pickering Dodge Allen, son of John Fisk Allen, Esq., of this city.

This adds one more to the list of Northern young men of promise who have offered themselves up as patriotic sacrifices on the altar of their country, and whose memories should be ever tenderly cherished. Being possessed of a fortune which rendered him independent, young Allen had visited nearly every part of the world, and was engaged in an extended European tour when the news of the war reached him in a foreign country. He immediately cut short his proposed excursion, returned home, and with his patriotic ardor, unrestrained by considerations of fortune, home comforts, or social relations, enlisted in the service.

He was commissioned as a Lieutenant in the First Unattached Company of Cavalry in Captain Read's Squadron of Mounted Rifle Rangers, and served with that Corps in Louisiana. He was subsequently appointed Senior Aid-de-Camp on Brigadier-General Weitzel's Staff. His gallantry on several occasions has been duly noted, and his bravery on board the gunboat Diana, and in the capture of the rebel steamer Cornie, will be well remembered. In the former of these encounters he was severely wounded, and probably had not entirely recovered from the effects of the wound when he was seized with the malarial fever, of which he died at Brashear City. He was about twenty-five years old.

[From the Salem Gazette, June 16—Editorial.]

The afflictive intelligence of the death of Lieutenant PICKERING DODGE ALLEN, of this city, which was received on Saturday last, not only cast a gloom over a very large circle of personal and family friends, but was felt by the public as a loss to the country of a brave soldier and gallant leader. Here, in the place of his birth, and where all his home life had been passed, his kind disposition and amiable deportment had won the general regard, while the manly and heroic qualities developed by active service, in the camp and on the field of battle, had given him a place in the public respect which many years of peaceful life and successful money-getting would have failed to secure.

The breaking out of the rebellion found him abroad, engaged in completing a very extensive course of travel, including the great East India marts, to which he had been impelled perhaps by his commercial descent. But the spirit of patriotism was too strong in him to permit his continuance in any pursuits in which the safety and welfare of the country and the institutions which he loved were subordinate to mere personal pleasure, improvement or profit. He hastened home, and at once began to look around for the best way to make himself useful in the public service. It was not long before the commission of lieutenant of cavalry was offered him by General Butler, and he at once proceeded with energy and perseverance to fill up his company by enlistments, and to fit himself for the novel duties with which he was charged. How well he succeeded has been since proved on more than one occasion by the strain of extremest trial. The unfortunate conflict of authority between Governor Andrew and General Butler, in which the War Department seems to have been most in fault, led to his virtual supersedure while in active service at New Orleans, and he came home for a brief period,—not, however, to retire in disgust from a service in which he felt he had been ill used, but to put himself in a position in which he might honorably return to the service. This was speedily effected, and he returned to New Orleans, where he was welcomed by the gallant General Weitzel, and received from him the appointment of Aid-de-Camp, and in this responsible position he continued, a member of the General's military family, until the end of his life.

We have not the means at hand to go with particularity into the details of Lieutenant Allen's military services. Very early in his career he had the honor of a special official mention—in the report of General Strong to General Butler of the attempt to surprise and capture Ponchatoula—for "having rendered important service and gallantry during action." The wound which probably led to his death was received in the defence of the gunboat Diana, on the twenty-eighth of March last, in which he displayed extraordinary gallantry and daring courage. He had of right no command in the boat, being a passenger, sent by General Weitzel for the purpose of gaining important military information. The commander of the Diana, disregarding the advice of Lieutenant Allen, got her into a disadvantageous position, where he was surprised and attacked by a superior force of the rebels. After the captain and all the executive officers of the boat had been killed or wounded, Lieutenant Allen took command, but found it impossible to get the sailors any longer to stand to the guns, and himself raised the Union flag again after they had hauled it down. At last, however, finding the insubordination such that it was impossible to have the guns loaded, and being severely wounded, he was reluctantly compelled to surrender.

He was treated with great kindness and attention by the rebels of the neighborhood in which he was captured—in consideration, as they said, of the kindness and forbearance with which he had treated them in some flag-of-truce business which he had previously had with them—and his wounds were healing rapidly, when he had a new experience, described in the New Orleans Picayune of April twenty-first, as follows:—

" When the Confederate forces commenced their retreat, several steamers started from Franklin to New Iberia, among them the Cornie, having on board her crew and about seventy wounded confederates. Lieutenant Allen, of General Weitzel's Staff, who was wounded and captured at the time the Diana was taken, was also on board with a guard, being conveyed to New Iberia as a prisoner. The captain of the Cornie appears to have been panic stricken, for he returned with his boat to Franklin, when Lieutenant Allen walked up into the town. At this time the Federal advance of cavalry occupied the place, and Lieutenant Allen, procuring a six-shooter from one of them, walked back on board the boat, and going up to the captain presented the pistol and demanded the surrender of the boat, which was at once complied with. Thus a good steamer, with nearly one hundred prisoners, fell into the hands of the Federal forces,

13

through the coolness and determination of one man. The confederates neglected to parole Lieutenant Allen; they merely put him upon the limits of the town, and he was consequently recaptured. He is now in New Orleans, and his wound is healing rapidly, so much so that he will be able to resume his duties on the staff in about ten days or two weeks. He speaks in high terms of the kindness and consideration with which he was treated while in the hands of the confederates."

The next we hear of Lieutenant Allen is the following:—

"A letter dated at Chicot Lake, Louisiana, May first, states that Lieutenant Pickering Dodge Allen of Salem was in command of steamer Cornie, with a section of artillery, two brass howitzers, and one hundred sharp-shooters from the Massachusetts Fourth Regiment, bound up the Atchafalaya River to the mouth of Red River to communicate with Admiral Farragut. The Cornie, it will be remembered, was a rebel steamer on which Lieutenant Allen was a prisoner, and was surrendered to him upon his demand when General Banks' expedition proved successful at Brashear City. Lieutenant Allen, who is a cavalry officer, was forbidden by the surgeon to rejoin his staff at present, as his wounds, although doing well, were not sufficiently healed to allow of saddle exercise, and so he obtained command of the Cornie, one of the vessels in Commodore Cooke's little fleet, which passed through the Atchafalaya to the mouth of Red River and brought down Admiral Farragut, who was at New Orleans at last advices. It is not often that a dragoon would find himself at home on shipboard, but Lieutenant Allen has had considerable experience at sea, having visited the East Indies, Japan, the California Coast, and nearly all parts of the world. His gallantry has been proved on several memorable occasions."

Subsequently, about a fortnight ago, a letter was received by his father, stating that the state of his health was such, that the physicians directed his return home, for recovery, and that he should accordingly return immediately. The next intelligence was the afflictive and unexpected news of his death.

It is probable that Lieutenant Allen was in the incipient stages of the malarial fever at the time of his writing. This terminated in typhoid, of which he died, at Brashear City, where he was surrounded by kind friends, and had every attention and aid which his situation required. His body will be brought to Salem for interment. His last letter was dated May twenty-sixth. His death occurred on the second of June.

[From the Essex Statesman, Salem, June 17—Editorial.]

We announce with pain the death of Lieutenant PICKERING DODGE ALLEN of Salem.

Lieutenant Allen went out with General Butler in the autumn of 1861, as lieutenant of a cavalry company, which he, with much labor and expense, helped to raise. When Governor Andrew issued commissions to the officers of General Butler's troops, the claims of Lieutenant Allen were overlooked; a private was appointed in his place; he was mustered out and returned to his home last summer. He was appointed a lieutenant in another company, and though the place was not the one he desired, and unequal to his deserts, still his heart was in the service and the cause, and after a short visit with his family, he returned to New Orleans in August last. He was soon detached from his command, and appointed on the staff of General Weitzel, and there continued till his death. He served with great distinction in several engagements, was captured in the steamer Diana and severely wounded. He had nearly recovered from his wounds, but a fever followed, and by the last letters from him, May twenty-sixth, he was to leave for home on a furlough. His family was daily expecting his return, when on Saturday last the sad and appalling news of his death reached them. A relapse of his fever was too much for his weakened powers, and he died.

We have sent from this city many of our best young men; we have lost many by battle and disease; but we can truly say that we have sent none whose future was more full of promise; we could have lost none whose death will be more sincerely mourned by all who knew him, not only as a personal and private affliction, but as a public loss.

We all remember with what zeal and spirit he entered upon his career.

Fond of adventure, addicted to out-door and manly exercises, filled with an earnest wish to do something for his country, and to respond to the call that the public peril made upon her young men, he was fitted by nature, by habit, and by moral purpose, for a soldier's life in this great struggle.

He was gentle, yet firm and manly; he was quiet, modest and unobtrusive, yet in the hour of danger he had enough of decision and self-assertion; he was well-principled and high-toned, and amid the fierce excesses of a soldier's life he kept the faith and honor of a gentleman, and has left a record without stain or reproach.

His circumstances were such that a less decided nature would have been prevented from adopting the career to which he devoted himself, and to which he gave his life. Born to wealth, surrounded by tender ties of friends, kindred and home, he turned from a life of comfort, opulence and inglorious ease, to the rough dangers of camp and battle-field; his manhood and his adventurous spirit there found the arena and the prize he coveted.

There is much in his character and his brief career to admire, and as we reflect upon them we find much to console and reconcile. We feel that his heroic qualities were not sapped by fortune, but were strong and ready for use in trial; we feel though he reached only the threshold of life, and fell exhausted at the open door, and saw honor and usefulness within, still it was not all in vain he lived and died.

He achieved much in life; he has left as much in death, —the memory of a brave, manly and true heart, which we shall tenderly cherish; the example of a gallant and generous sacrifice, which the young men of the Republic should now and henceforth emulate and copy.

The thunders of artillery and the roar of distant battle again rock the land and sea; other heroic spirits are hastening to join our cherished and beloved dead. God grant that the lives they give and the sharp grief that those who love them feel, may at last find recompense and consolation, in the restoration of our dear country to order, unity and peace.

11*

[From the Salem Gazette, June 23]

No city in our Commonwealth has more largely shared
in the hopes and fears of the terrible war, now devastating
the once fair portions of the land and burdening the loyal
hearts of the nation, than Salem; and to the sacred cause
she has freely given of her bravest and best. From those
gallent pioneers, the Salem Zouaves, in whose hearts the
first call to arms awoke an echo ever rolling on with each
succeeding conflict to the present hour, when "our boys"
have stretched forth a ready hand to aid a sister State, there
has been no check to the devotion of our young heroes, no
lull in the song of Freedom surging up from patriotic
hearts;—to the "music of the Union" they have marched
to glory, and they have found it often in the grave. The
debt of gratitude which all good citizens owe their country
has been paid in honorable wounds, shattered health and
gift of precious life; and still, as occasion demands, they go,
taking with them our farewells laden with blessings, claim-
ing hearty welcome on their return, or earning a hallowed
place in our memories.

And now another soldier has fought his last fight,—not
this time on the battle field, but as one might yield at home
to the universal conqueror Death. Kind hands ministered
to his last needs, and we rejoice that this great consolation
was granted to his friends.

All who have followed the footsteps of PICKERING
DODGE ALLEN, through his modest, conscientious and
gallant career, know that he has done his country good
service, and feel that a life ended in such a cause, although

cut short, is not lost. He *gave* it, and when we have so often said "God bless him" for his promptness in action, for his steadfast perseverance, for his dauntless courage, we did not know that God would so soon bless him in his own best way.

Life's warfare for him is over, and while we consecrate to his name a wreath of undying laurels, let us not repine because his youthful brow was deemed worthy of the amaranth crown in the realms of everlasting peace.

The first alarm of war found young Allen in the full enjoyment of an European tour, but true to himself and his country, he obeyed her call, and sought and obtained opportunity for service which he has ever made honorable by his conduct.

He survived a severe wound received in action which gained him high and merited praise, and sunk under a fever induced by too speedy return to the duties he was so eager to fulfil.

Yet not only as a soldier was our young townsman worthy of esteem;—a kind friend, affectionate brother, devoted son, —modest, simple, honest, straightforward,—developing many sturdy traits of the good old puritan families from which he was descended,—we find a warrant in saying that few young men were richer in well-wishers and friends. His cordial greeting will be listened for in vain by those to whom he was ever welcome, and over the circle of immediate friends a shadow has fallen that will not soon be dispelled. To the stricken household, to the parents who have guided him from a fragile infancy to a manhood full of promise, the bereavement is almost heart-breaking. That God may comfort them in this great sorrow is the prayer of many a sympathizing heart.   s.

At a special meeting of the City Council on Thursday evening, Thomas Nichols, Jr., Esq., presiding, in absence of Mr. Choate, Mayor Wheatland sent in a message concerning Lieutenant Allen's death, which was referred to a joint special committee, consisting of Aldermen Pickman and Webster, and Councilmen Perry, White and Clark, who reported resolutions which we print below. The Mayor's letter was as follows:—

"CITY OF SALEM.

"*Mayor's Office, June* 18, 1863.

"GENTLEMEN OF THE CITY COUNCIL,—

"The remains of our late fellow citizen, Lieutenant PICKERING DODGE ALLEN, have been received by his friends, and the last tribute of respect will be paid to them on Friday afternoon.

"His family are very decided that the funeral shall be private, but at the same time are willing that all who feel an interest in him should be present.

"Lieutenant Allen was a personal friend, one whom I have known for many years, and I hardly dare to trust myself to speak of him; but I feel that his heroism and devotion to his country are known to all of us, and that we can cordially unite in saying that this terrible struggle has taken very few who will be more sincerely mourned, or who have left a brighter example to his country.

"No one has left his home from purer and more patriotic motives, and no one has borne himself, among the temptations and trials of the camp, more like a true gentleman and soldier."

The following resolutions were unanimously adopted, having been previously spoken to by Mr. Perry, who alluded very handsomely to the high character of Lieutenant Allen, as a representative of the intelligence and patriotism of our city:—

"*Whereas,* The painful intelligence of the death of Lieutenant PICKERING DODGE ALLEN, on the second day of June, 1863, at Brashear City, in the State of Louisiana, in the twenty-fifth year of his age, while serving upon the staff of General Weitzel, has been officially communicated to us by his Honor the Mayor, therefore

"*Resolved,* That in all our losses in this calamitous war, the city has suffered no greater loss. We remember with patriotic pride the zeal with which he entered upon the service of his country in the day of its peril. We recall his gentle, modest and unobtrusive, yet firm and manly bearing. We know that his singular purity of character preserved to him, amid the trying scenes of camp and field, the faith and honor of a gentleman and a soldier. We mourn his early death, not only as a private affliction, but as a public calamity. The city will cherish his memory as that of a brave and true man, and his example will remain for emulation and praise.

"*Resolved,* That the City Council will attend his funeral in a body.

"*Resolved,* That the communication of his Honor the Mayor, together with these resolutions, be entered at length upon the records of the city, and copies of them be sent to the parents of Lieutenant Allen, with the deepest sympathy of the city in this hour of their bereavement."

The funeral services, at the house of J. Fisk Allen, Esq., father of the deceased, were of a private character, but were attended by a great number of people. The City Government were present, and the members of the Salem Light Infantry, and numerous private and personal friends of the deceased. The services were conducted by Rev. Dr. Briggs. The flags of the city were displayed at half mast, and the bells tolled, as a token of respect for the deceased.

At a meeting of the Salem Light Infantry, held at their armory on Friday, General George H. Devereux in the chair, the following resolutions were passed:—

"It has pleased Providence to take from our old corps yet another victim of this destructive war. Lieutenant Pickering Dodge Allen has died from disease resulting from wounds received in the gallant discharge of his duties to his country. Like many another generous and brave spirit nurtured in our military organization, he staked his life upon the perils of these troubled times in support of the free institutions and endangered interests of his native land.

"Hastening home from abroad at the first anticipation of this momentous struggle, he sought eagerly the opportunity to uphold the cause of the violated Constitution and the insulted Flag of the United States, and voluntarily left a position of ease and independence, blest with every social advantage, to undergo the hardships and face the dangers of warfare.

"Circumstances offered him the opportunity to prove, amid trying difficulty and pressing danger, the earnestness of his patriotism and the unyielding energy of his spirit; and in the hour of emergency, he displayed the high qualities and the enduring courage that can redeem misfortune and turn failure into victory. But the wounds received in battle, and too much neglected in his eagerness to resume his duties, induced the fatal disease that has terminated his young and honorable life. The shouts of well won triumph and the tears of grieving comrades mingled around his distant death bed, and his lifeless form has been transmitted to his home—all that is now left to his friends of the young and chivalrous patriot soldier.

"Therefore *Resolved*, That we tender to his parents and family our deep commiseration for the early loss of one, in whom so much of hope and earthly expectation was treasured up; and we pray that the cheering memory of duty nobly done, and the purest consolations of Divine wisdom may support and comfort their affliction.

"*Resolved*, That with a sad and proud satisfaction, we place his name upon that already long and honorable roll of our comrades who have sealed with their lives their manly devotion to duty; and given to our corps a distinction and preëminence in the annals of this bloody war, which will be cherished by all who have ever worn, or shall wear, in after times, the uniform of the Salem Light Infantry. Peaceful be his rest in his early, but glorious tomb. And may the God of battles shield from harm the gallant band of our surviving brothers still clustered round the banners of the republic.

"*Resolved*, That a copy of these resolutions be entered upon the record of the corps, and that a copy be transmitted to the family of the deceased."

[From the Salem Gazette, June 30.]

The subjoined tribute to the memory of the lamented Lieutenant ALLEN has been forwarded to us for publication by Captain S. Tyler Read:—

"HEAD-QUARTERS MOUNTED RIFLE RANGERS,

"HUMPHREY'S STATION,

"*Parish St. James, La., June* 10, 1863.

"GENERAL ORDERS NO. 15.

The Captain Commanding announces with profound sadness the death of First Lieutenant Pickering Dodge Allen of this Company, and Senior Aid-de-Camp to Brigadier-General Weitzel.

"This event, which we, and all who knew our good and brave Lieutenant, must so deeply mourn, occurred at Brashear City, Louisiana, on the second instant. He had fought with such defiant bravery in the very breath of the enemy's guns at Pattersonville, on the twenty-eighth of March, that at last when captured, severely wounded in several places, his shot-honored garments hanging about him in shreds and the men he had urged to desperate fight strewn around him, even his enemies, in admiration of his bravery, heaped upon him extravagant praises and unaccustomed courtesies.

"Afterwards, while yet in the hands of the enemy and suffering from his wounds, the enthusiasm with which he saw the glorious flag he had loved and honored advancing at the head of our forces nerved him with strength to rise from his couch, demand the unconditional surrender of the hospital steamboat on which he was confined, and bring it, loaded with rebels, a trophy to the Federal forces. Too fatally fond of his country's fame and cause, before he had wholly recovered from the effects of his wounds or was again fit for the hardships of the field, he heard the sounds of approaching battle and could not be restrained from resuming his duties upon his General's Staff; sickness and that sad event which we deplore followed.

"We may not here allude to his previous and valuable services in his country's cause; he sleeps proudly now beneath the national emblem he has given his life to redeem from insult.

"We who knew him mourn the true and noble-hearted gentleman, the faithful and affectionate friend, the pure and devoted patriot, the gallant and heroic soldier! And it is ordered that the Company's colors and the officers' quarters shall be trimmed in mourning, that the members of the Company shall wear the usual badge for thirty days, and that a copy of this order shall be forwarded to the parents of the deceased as a testimonial of our respect and love for the memory of their lamented son.

"By order, S. TYLER READ,

"Captain Commanding Mounted Rifle Rangers,

"Independent Massachusetts Volunteers."

14

A

SERMON

DELIVERED IN SALEM, JUNE 21, 1863,

By REV. G. W. BRIGGS, D. D.

SERMON.

—

REVELATIONS XX., 12.

"AND ANOTHER BOOK WAS OPENED, WHICH IS THE BOOK OF LIFE."

I think of no sentence which can more fitly introduce our meditations to-day. I think of none which, at the same time, touches such profound spiritual truths and finds such vivid illustrations in the events of the hour. The writer is speaking of the future, and not of the present world. He is attempting to picture the grand and awful scenes which presented themselves to his imagination in his visions of a spiritual state. But the change of worlds can neither suspend nor break the laws of the soul. For what is the "Book of Life"? What idea is that consecrated phrase intended to convey? Does not the "book of life" mean, the principle of man's inward being, that which he truly is in his *interior character* before the sight of God? And is not that book opened whenever that principle is brought out into view? Though the text was written concerning the

14*

future, it belongs to the present also. It describes
the work both of Time and of Eternity. The book
of life is not kept closed and sealed until the dawn of
a judgment day. Though it may not be fully opened
here, seal after seal is unloosed in the events which
produce genuine revelations of character. Sometimes it seems as if few seals remained to be broken
when the spirit passes on into that higher world to
whose glories the text directly refers. Let us follow
this line of thought, first, in the general reflections
which it suggests, and then into such particular applications as the time may permit.

"And another book was opened, which is the book
of life." It is the grand office of experience to reveal
the moral secrets of the heart, to open the book of life.
Everything that stirs the soul, indeed, reveals a glimpse
of the inner life, even if none of its features are fully
unveiled. Its pride, its passion, its selfishness, or, its
humility, its heroism, its love, are constantly flashing
into sight amidst the provocations and the tasks of life.
The true tones of feeling break from the heart when
the different events of life touch its various strings, I
had almost said as surely, and oftentimes as unconsciously, as the different notes of the organ when you
touch its various stops and keys. The book of life
is partially opened every day. I am entering into no

mere speculations now. I am writing what you and I have felt ofttimes in humiliation, and perhaps in tears, and sometimes, I trust, in joy. What secrets of weakness, and what secrets of strength, experience opens! What secrets of weakness, certainly! Who has never found that a new or varied temptation, a provocation unmet before, has shaken, if not over-whelmed his fancied heroism of purpose? The serenity in which you trusted yielded at the first assault, and the passion which you thought you had tamed, or could hold in check, breaks out again in all its wonted strength. Somehow the old demon comes back again when you believed that the cham-bers of the heart had been swept and garnished, or else some new weakness appears, which was undis-covered before, to keep you still humble when you began to feel the pride of spiritual strength and victory. When you think you can walk upon the stormy waves, like the too confident Apostle you begin to sink, and are compelled to cry for the help of the Master's hand. I know not how any man can be a Pharisee. He could not be if he read the opening book of life. Fall upon your knees, and smite your breast, sooner than breathe one word, or thought of spiritual pride, as these secrets of frailty come into view to shame and humble you.

But thanks be given, there is another side to the picture. Life opens secrets of strength as well as of weakness. Resolution does not always bend beneath assaults. Sometimes it has an invincible and adamantine firmness that no experience in life is able to shake. Sometimes serenity is undisturbed, and loving souls retain their sweetness, while the excitements of passion are heaving and tossing round them in perpetual agitation. If any angel has found a home in the spirit, either implanted there by the love that watched over and guided its opening life, or developed by the soul's earnest struggles to keep its faith and honor, under difficulties and temptations it will unfold its previously secret and unsuspected strength. Have you never found such an inward strength in the conviction instilled, perhaps, by a mother's lips, the sentiment awakened by her counsel or her presence,—a strength that you never claimed as your own but always gratefully attributed to her, but which kept you as clean from the sins against which she specially warned you, long after she was laid in the grave, as if her loving arms were folded round you still? Have you not seen such an inward strength winning its moral victories in other souls? Experience probes the heart's hidden places and opens the books of the spirit's life to tell its secrets of shame or glory.

"And another book was opened, which is the book
of life." When I follow out this line of thought
the intensest experiences of life involve no mystery.
Their explanation is seen at a glance. They open
the books of life more fully. They sound the depths
of character. They expose the latent frailty which
nothing less would reveal, or they call out the latent
strength which no lighter summons would arouse.
Man does not need the merely superficial experiences
which bring no disappointment, and can demand no
trust; which ask for no self-sacrifice, and can sum-
mon up no heroism. He needs those which are as
deep as the heart's capacities of love; deep as the
possibilities of spiritual frailty, or of spiritual power.
They have their compensations. They surprise us
by the displays of character to which they lead.
Sometimes, too often, human nature sinks beneath
its grandest tests. But now and then it rises to a
moral power that is equal to the demand upon its
strength, and ascends to a true spiritual victory.
What are these manifestations of trust, and of power?
They are partial openings of the book of life. We
begin to read some of the pages of that wondrous
book in these grander revelations of character. Some
souls pass through the years of present life, unknown
to others, unknown even to themselves. Nothing

comes to arouse the grander elements of their spiritual nature, and it gives no sign of its diviner possibilities. Not even once, perhaps, in all their earthly history do they have a single hour of transfiguration, in which the soul breaks through the features to cover them with light and the inner man comes out in a heroism, or a self-sacrifice that fills us with admiration, and almost with reverence. How many talents sleep till the angel of the resurrection shall call them forth into glorious activity? I often think of the infinite surprises that will come to myriads of souls, in the intenser life of the future, when these powers which scarcely budded here shall burst into bloom,—when those who were chained below by man's injustice, or the unfavorable circumstances of their present lot, shall see their prison walls falling round them and pass into the liberty of the heavens, —when those who grovelled here on earth as if they were only made of the dust, quickly to return to dust again, shall find the spirit putting forth its wings to soar up towards the life of God. "Neither eye hath seen, nor ear heard, nor heart conceived" what those surprises may be. Still, occasionally, when life is deepest, we get glimpses of that unrevealed, uncomprehended splendor. Occasionally we see revelations of glorious manhood which illuminate the dark pages of human history, and shine down through the centuries to cheer and inspire. Occasionally the heavens seem to open and a still more spiritual baptism rests upon some saintly head. It is the deep experiences that open the book of life. I do not wonder that they come. I cannot wonder at the agony which finally leads to the cry, "Thy will be done." I wonder not at the heavy cross which may make the soul its conqueror at last. The dark cloud of sorrow is already fringed with light. I see the meaning of the words, "Whom he loveth, he chasteneth." The still darker problem of moral evil is not wholly mystery. Though itself unsolved, some light is cast upon it now. Life is a battle; truth brings not peace, but a sword; every step towards the world's progress and redemption is purchased by sacrifices of blood, because in these tremendous moral struggles the book of life may be opened, and all that is great in heroism, all that is sublime in love and trust, all that is glorious in self-sacrifice may be written upon its pages.

And shall I turn from this abstract and general statement to its illustrations in the life of to-day? How nobly character has been developed amidst these terrible convulsions! I do not forget for an instant the manifestations of moral weakness, the disastrous failures which sadden us, the selfishness which never rises above its own base and personal ends when all that is sacred and dear in the thought of country, and law, and liberty is pleading with its heart of stone, and which is as unmoved by any true enthusiasm for interests so divine as was the heart of Judas by love for his Lord.   Like the traitor himself it must go to its own place, and I put it out of sight to-day.   Thanks for the true and brave, those whose bravery and truth can almost make us forget these shameful lives.   How many youths whose moral power we could not have realized, and perhaps did not suspect, have suddenly developed into the noblest manhood, with a loyalty to liberty exalted into a soul of self-sacrifice, and the love of country kindled into a quenchless flame?   When has the book of life been more truly opened to reveal the deeps of character?   When have nobler things been written upon its pages?   We almost imagine amidst such abundant manifestations of heroism and devotion that they are the positive creations of the hour, as if some new inspiration had been poured upon humanity to-day. A new inspiration has indeed come; but it has created nothing.   It has simply opened the book of its interior life, to show us what it was made to be when it yields itself without reserve to a sacred truth or a

noble sentiment. Heroism, fidelity, devotion, are as
natural to such self-sacrificing natures as cowardice
and moral treason to self-seeking souls. These
grander things are the natural expression of this
nobler, inward life. It is sometimes said that these
beautiful developments of character are the only compensations in this terrific war. Other issues are not
yet unveiled. I leave those in faith to the guidance
of the overruling Hand. But here are compensations
which come while other, and grander ones if that be
possible, are still unseen,—compensations which outweigh suffering, yes, almost outweigh grief itself.
We should not have known these heroes except
through the perils amidst which they nobly battled,
and bravely fell. I gather up these bright revelations out of the book of their life. I count the
names that have become sacred now. Who that
felt rightly would deem any peril or cross a burden
to himself if it should imbue him with the true soul
of sacrifice? In our better moments we say with
Paul, we would know the fellowship of the Lord's
sufferings, and taste the bitterness of his death, if
thus, by any means, we might attain to a resurrection
from the dead. Shall we put our personal griefs,
however sacred and deep, into the balance, when we
remember these examples of moral beauty? We will

15

open our clinging arms to let our beloved ones go. Tearfully, yet bravely, we will bear a suffering, a sacrifice, like that from which they did not shrink, and which made them what they were, and what they must be in our memory forever.

And here another thought presses upon the mind. We have said that the deep things of character, its diviner forces, are called forth amidst these tremendous experiences. If life open the book of character, death cannot close it. It seems to open it still more widely. It is an unfailing and beautiful office of death to bring character up anew to the mind and heart. Well did Jesus say to the disciples that the Spirit would bring all things to their remembrance when he should have gone away. It was in accordance with the irresistible working of human nature. Then the mind goes back to the past, and the heart gathers up and embalms its cherished and beautiful memories. And how those memories throng upon it; recollections of every generous and characteristic deed,—recollections to which we seldom turned, and which had almost faded, but which now come up, fresh and vivid, to bear their testimony. When the life is really lovely and true we are compassed about as by a cloud of these loving witnesses. The heart calls all things to its remembrance, and groups them together to make the portrait complete, as the loving painter touches each feature again and yet again with his magic pencil, until the picture assumes the exact expression and hues of life. Death cannot close the book of life. The features of the spirit are never so distinct as when the veil of flesh is laid aside. It sometimes seems as if the truest ministry of the loved begins when their earthly presence ceases. Then superficial foibles are forever blotted out, and the nobler qualities appear without a cloud. Then the traits which formerly seemed so beautiful assume a sacredness unknown before, and the once human life fulfils the office of an angel. Perhaps the lips never speak so eloquently as when they are closed forever. Perhaps no life is ever truly known, certainly none exerts its highest spiritual power till it is ended. How true it is in every application of the words that those who live can never die! When character is true death is indeed abolished, and the mortal life becomes an immortal presence, to touch the soul with a tenderer reverence and sway it with a diviner power. When the book of life is truly opened, life and death alike conspire to illuminate its pages, and make them radiant forever.

I do not forget the anguish and agony of the hour in words like these. Certainly I cannot forget them

when I hear so often the sadly tolling bells. I see
the loved forms of the dead coming back so silently
to be laid by the side of parents and of kindred. It
is because the sacrifices are so priceless that I strive
to gather every gleam of consolation and of hope.
How oft it seems as if our most single-hearted and
truest fell! When the devotion is most nobly
proved; when the young man to whom life opened
with fairest promise, offering every charm to hold
him back, hears the call of country across the sea and
hastens to her defence; when character retains its
simplicity, its integrity, its honor undefiled amidst
the corruptions of the camp, to command a confidence
and love from former strangers almost as tender and
deep as the affections of home; when the hopes of
kindred and of associates begin to cluster round it
as if reserved for marked and nobler service to the
sacred cause; when the sacrifice seems greatest, then
the call comes to withhold it not. " Withhold not
thy son, thine only son." It is the law of the eter-
nal Providence. It was the offering without spot or
blemish that was to be placed upon the altars. It is
the fairest and most priceless lives that seem oftenest
laid down for right and for humanity. Sacrifices
like these have the highest moral power, and do
most to touch and quicken sluggish and selfish souls.

When their work seems so sadly and mysteriously ended, it is that they may begin their nobler work in the deep places of human hearts. We gain some partial solution of their early fall. Those who have the moral power of character pass on to exert an inspiration, which, though unseen, nerves a hundred hearts anew, and is mightier, a thousand fold, than any mortal strength.

"And another book was opened, which is the book of life." Our text might suggest a higher and more spiritual doctrine, at which we cannot even glance to-day. Let us fill our minds with these thoughts of hope. When the book of life is truly opened, and character shines forth in its moral beauty, we have a power that cannot die. It neither dies in human memory, nor in its influence upon the world. Shall this grand heroism that is covering the land with patriot graves fail to do its work? Should it fail to-day, it would only make them shrines to which men would turn in some future time for inspiration; and the sacrifice which is unavailing now will purchase a redemption in the coming centuries. Not one loyal man can live or die in vain. The truths which such men serve, at the cost of sacrifice and life, seem more real and precious for every new offering in their defence. The words "Country" and

"Liberty" have new sacredness and power when we see what inspirations they shed down upon these brave and generous souls. We catch the inspiration too, and feel that there is nothing better than to enter into heroic life of faith and sacrifice. And then, once more, this opening of the books of life is the opening of the heavens. Whenever we see life, we instantly believe in immortality. We do not merely believe, we feel, we know, that love, truth, purity, can never die. The memories of human virtue are the assurances of heaven. We instinctively look beyond the grave when we are called to look down with deepest sadness into its silence. Thanks for the light of immortality that shines through the gates of the tomb as the best beloved are passing on. Let it brighten upon our faith till it break upon our sight forevermore.

www.ingramcontent.com/pod-product-compliance
Lightning Source LLC
Chambersburg PA
CBHW031115020726
47495CB00007B/2207

* 9 7 8 3 3 3 7 0 9 3 8 5 3 *